Acting Edition

Dracula: A Comedy of Terrors

by Gordon Greenberg
and Steve Rosen

very loosely based on the novel
Dracula by Bram Stoker

No one shall make any changes in this title(s) for the purpose of production. No part of this book may be reproduced, stored in a retrieval system, scanned, uploaded, or transmitted in any form, by any means, now known or yet to be invented, including mechanical, electronic, digital, photocopying, recording, videotaping, or otherwise, without the prior written permission of the publisher. No one shall share this title(s), or any part of this title(s), through any social media or file hosting websites.

For all inquiries regarding motion picture, television, online/digital and other media rights, please contact Concord Theatricals Corp.

MUSIC AND THIRD-PARTY MATERIALS USE NOTE

Licensees are solely responsible for obtaining formal written permission from copyright owners to use copyrighted music and/or other copyrighted third-party materials (e.g. artworks, logos) in the performance of this play and are strongly cautioned to do so. If no such permission is obtained by the licensee, then the licensee must use only original music and materials that the licensee owns and controls. Licensees are solely responsible and liable for clearances of all third-party copyrighted materials, including without limitation music, and shall indemnify the copyright owners of the play(s) and their licensing agent, Concord Theatricals Corp., against any costs, expenses, losses and liabilities arising from the use of such copyrighted third-party materials by licensees. For music, please contact the appropriate music licensing authority in your territory for the rights to any incidental music.

IMPORTANT BILLING AND CREDIT REQUIREMENTS

If you have obtained performance rights to this title, please refer to your licensing agreement for important billing and credit requirements.

DRACULA: A COMEDY OF TERRORS was commissioned and originally produced by The Maltz Jupiter Theatre (Andrew Kato, Producing Artistic Director/Chief Executive) in Jupiter, Florida, and had its world premiere there on October 31st, 2019. The production was directed by Gordon Greenberg, with scenic design by Caite Hevner, costume design by Tristan Raines, lighting design by Rob Denton, sound design by Victoria Deiorio, and wig and hair design by Ashley Rae Callahan. The Production Stage Manager was Ashley Horowitz. The cast was as follows:

ACTOR ONE (JONATHAN HARKER) . . . . .Peter Simon Hilton
ACTOR TWO (DR. WESTFELDT). Wayne LeGette
ACTOR THREE (LUCY WESTFELDT) . . . . Mallory Newbrough
ACTOR FOUR (MINA WESTFELDT/DR. VAN HELSING). . . . Paul Carlin
ACTOR FIVE (DRACULA) . . . . .Jared Zirilli

DRACULA: A COMEDY OF TERRORS made its Canadian premiere at the Segal Centre for the Performing Arts (Lisa Rubin, Artistic and Executive Director) in Montréal, Québec, on October 29th, 2021. The production was directed by Gordon Greenberg, with scenic design by Michael Gianfrancesco, costume design by Louise Bourret, lighting design by Amber Hood, sound and original music by Victoria Deiorio. The Production Stage Manager was Elaine Normandeau. The cast was as follows:

ACTOR ONE (JONATHAN HARKER) . . . . Colin Simmons
ACTOR TWO (DR. WESTFELDT). . . . . Ellen David
ACTOR THREE (LUCY WESTFELDT) . . . . Naomi Ngebulana
ACTOR FOUR (MINA WESTFELDT/DR. VAN HELSING). . . . David Noël
ACTOR FIVE (DRACULA) . . . . .James Daly

DRACULA: A COMEDY OF TERRORS was originally produced in New York City by Drew Desky and Dane Levens (Drew & Dane Productions), and opened at New World Stages on September 18th, 2023. The production was directed by Gordon Greenberg, with scenic design by Tijana Bjelajac, costume design by Tristan Raines, lighting design by Rob Denton, sound design by Victoria Deiorio, and wig and hair design by Ashley Rae Callahan. The Production Stage Manager was Morgan Holbrook. The cast was as follows:

ACTOR ONE (JONATHAN HARKER) . . . . .Andrew Keenan-Bolger
ACTOR TWO (DR. WESTFELDT). . . . . Ellen Harvey
ACTOR THREE (LUCY WESTFELDT) . . . . .Jordan Boatman
ACTOR FOUR (MINA WESTFELDT/DR. VAN HELSING). . Arnie Burton
ACTOR FIVE (DRACULA) . . . . .James Daly

CHARACTERS

COUNT DRACULA – Commanding European dialect. Hugely sexy, magnetically handsome, rock star presence with a killer body, he is a narcissist whose greatest love is himself – and his leather pants. Bored with women falling all over him, he becomes obsessed with Lucy when he hears of her strength and adventurousness. The less she needs him, the more interested he is. He travels to Whitby to find her and make her his bride for eternity.

JONATHAN HARKER – RP British dialect. Prim and proper and obsessive-compulsive real estate agent, frightened of his own shadow. Engaged to his childhood crush Lucy Westfeldt and enamored of her fearlessness. Once bitten he loosens up...a lot... and becomes a Tom Jones-style rock star in leather pants.

LUCY WESTFELDT – RP British dialect. Brilliant, plucky earth scientist daughter of Dr. Westfeldt, she is full of energy and the spirit of adventure and often underestimated because of her beauty. Engaged to Jonathan, but when Dracula moves to Whitby, she is curious about his strange ways and impressed by their similar interests.

MINA WESTFELDT – RP British dialect. The less attractive, less intelligent Westfeldt daughter, she lives in her sister Lucy's shadow and is desperate for attention. She is immediately (pathetically) receptive to Dracula's charms.

DR. WALLACE WESTFELDT – RP British dialect. Lucy and Mina's father, a blowhard; self-important misogynist given to proclamations and posturing with his pipe. A doctor caring for the criminally insane, he has recently lost his wife to consumption.

DR. VAN HELSING – German dialect a la Mel Brooks. Brilliant and sturdy German vampire-hunting doctor from the University of Schmutz. Deadly serious in the way Germans can be, she is accustomed to people not believing she is a real doctor. Strong, shmart, unt bold, she is a woman of action.

RENFIELD – Cockney dialect and salivary issues. Insane patient of Dr. Westfeldt who lives to serve and loves to eat bugs. In a word, the dude is nuts.

KITTY RUTHERFORD – Cockney dialect. A dotty kleptomaniac patient of Dr. Westfeldt, she serves as a maid in his house. Think Mrs. Lovett but servile and easily distracted.

LORD CAVENDISH – Scottish dialect. Lucy's suitor; a Scottish dolt.

LORD WORTHINGTON – RP British dialect. Lucy's suitor; posh, British and petulant.

LORD HAVEMERCY – Texas Accent. Lucy's arrogant suitor from Memphis, a la Yosemite Sam.

DRIVER – Eastern European or Russian dialect. The male, Transylvanian driver of the carriage carrying Jonathan to Dracula's castle who tries to warn him. Borat meets Boris and Natasha.

CAPTAIN – Sea Captain dialect. The salty captain of a doomed ship caught in a raging storm.

BOSUN – Irish dialect. A scurvy seaman who goes down with the ship in a storm.

GRAVEDIGGER – Cockney dialect. A drunk gravedigger with a secret.

AUTHORS' NOTES

About Casting and Gender

Please note that the play lovingly sends up gender "norms" in the style of some of our comedic heroes like Charles Ludlam and Monty Python, in that all characters can be played by actors of any gender, ethnicity, age or type.

The breakdown of roles for the New York premiere at New World Stages was as indicated below.

ACTOR ONE – Harker/Cavendish/Worthington/Havemercy/Bosun/Gravedigger

ACTOR TWO – Dr. Westfeldt/Renfield/Captain/Man-Eating Wolf

ACTOR THREE – Lucy/Kitty/Driver/Man-Eating Wolf

ACTOR FOUR – Mina/Van Helsing/Man-Eating Wolf

ACTOR FIVE – Dracula

Prologue

(Music.)*

*(***ACTORS ONE, TWO, THREE** *and* **FOUR** *enter, each holding a book. In the style of the opening of James Whale's 1931 film* Frankenstein...)*

ACTOR TWO. Good evening.

ACTOR FOUR. On behalf of theater management we have been asked to issue a friendly warning.

ACTOR THREE. We're about to unfold the story of Dracula.

ACTOR ONE. A bloodthirsty monster who plays God with helpless victims.

ACTOR TWO. Draining them of life to extend his own.

ACTOR FOUR. It is one of the strangest tales ever told.

ACTOR THREE. It deals with the most significant aspects of the human condition.

ACTOR FOUR. Life –

ACTOR TWO. Death –

ACTOR ONE. And a hot guy who takes off his shirt. Heyyy!

ACTOR TWO. Although the novel is 418 pages, this evening's presentation will be significantly shorter.

(Woosh. They toss the books.)

ACTOR FOUR. You're welcome.

---

* A license to produce *DRACULA: A COMEDY OF TERRORS* does not include a performance license for any third-party or copyrighted recordings. Licensees should create their own.

ACTOR THREE. But rest assured you will be horrified.

ACTOR ONE. One way or another.

ACTOR FOUR. So if anyone here does not care to subject their nerves to such a strain, now is your chance to –

(Sound effects: Outer doors lock.)

Oh well, we warned you.

(Sound effects: Thunder clap, horses clopping, carriage wheels on the ground, wolves howling, loud wind –)

Scene One

(**ACTOR ONE** *dons a blazer and eyeglasses to become...***JONATHAN HARKER**, *and addresses the audience, speaking aloud his letter home to his fiancée. Meanwhile, two benches are adjusted to become a carriage, and* **ACTOR THREE** *dons a hat and cape to become the* **DRIVER**.)

HARKER. October the 5th, 1897. Dearest Lucy, apologies for my unsteady penmanship. I write to you from the inside of a carriage en route to my client's home in the mountains of Transylvania.

(*He sits in the "rear seat" of the carriage, and thrashes about [to indicate a very bumpy road], holds onto a briefcase, and shouts to the* **DRIVER** *over the wind.*)

Excuse me, driver? Any chance you could slow it down a smidge? This road is awfully bumpy, and with my chronic vertigo and digestive issues, I'm afraid I'm rather the worse for wear.

DRIVER. (*Transylvanian accent.*) This area is extremely treacherous.

HARKER. Oh yes, I've done my research, but I couldn't find any of these roads on the map!

DRIVER. Of course not. No one who travels here ever comes back.

(*Sound effects: Horses neigh loudly.*)

HARKER. Sorry?

DRIVER. There is nothing here but centuries of death, destruction and evil!

(*Sound effects: Horses neigh loudly.*)

HARKER. Are they alright, the horses?

DRIVER. Oh yes. I've trained them to punctuate my lines for dramatic effect.

> *(Sound effects: Horses neigh again.)*

Sometimes, they overdo it.

HARKER. Well I hope they've enough strength for the remainder of the journey because I have to get to the castle. I have urgent business with Count Dracula.

> *(Sound effects: Horses neigh loudly.)*

DRIVER. Count Dracula? I beg of you sir, heed my warning, do not enter that wretched castle!

HARKER. Well I can find something nice to say about any home. It's my job. I'm a real estate broker.

> *(Sound effects: Horses exhale. Clopping stops. Wind through trees.)*

Why have the horses stopped?

DRIVER. They sense danger. Must be the man-eating wolves. You'll have to walk the rest of the way.

HARKER. Walk?

DRIVER. It's not far, you'll probably make it.

> *(**HARKER** slowly exits the carriage.)*

HARKER. But what about the wolves?

DRIVER. Try this.

> *(**DRIVER** pulls a small braid of garlic from a hidden pocket and tosses it to **HARKER**.)*

HARKER. Garlic?

DRIVER. From the farmers market in Bucharest. God be with you, sir.

(Beat.)

And please...remember to give me five stars.

(Sound effects: Thunder. Lightning.)

ACTOR TWO. Jonathan Harker made his way through the Carpathian woods.

ACTOR FOUR. Where he could see the glow of yellow eyes through the trees.

> **(ACTORS TWO, THREE** *and* **FOUR** *hold light-up wolf eyes.)*

ACTOR THREE. Staring at him hungrily.

ACTOR FOUR. Growling with menace.

> **(ACTORS TWO, THREE** *and* **FOUR** *growl.)*

ACTOR THREE. He was terrified.

ACTOR FOUR. Like Margaret Thatcher at a dental convention.

ACTOR TWO. Just as the wolves were poised to attack.

> *(More growling.)*

HARKER. *(Terrified.)* Good doggy. Good doggy. Who's a good doggy? How about some fresh garlic, then?

> *(Sound effects: Whimpering wolves leaving.)*

(Calling after them.) Don't you want any? It's from the farmers market! Huh. How queer.

ACTOR TWO. With the path cleared, he made his way to the front door of the castle.

ACTOR THREE. He saw it through the fog...

> **(ACTORS TWO** *and* **THREE** *spray* **HARKER** *with fog in a can.)*

ACTOR THREE. ...a vast gothic structure with no windows.

ACTOR FOUR. So not a glimmer of light could be seen inside.

ACTOR TWO. And whose broken battlements showed a jagged line against the sky.

HARKER. I say, the driver was right, it *is* awfully creepy. I can see why he wants to move. Oh well, here goes...

(He extends his finger and rings the...)

(Sound effects: Doorbell.)

ACTOR TWO. And right there –

ACTOR THREE. Dressed entirely in black –

ACTOR TWO. Stood none other than –

(Sound effects: A door opens to reveal **COUNT DRACULA**, *a sexually-charged rock star of a vampire clad in tight pants and vest.)*

DRACULA. Count Dracula. Nice to meet you.

(Music: "Funky Vampire Theme." *)*

(He walks downstage, almost in semi-slow motion, as if walking a runway at Paris fashion week.)

*(***ACTORS THREE** and **FOUR** spray fog in a can toward him.)*

Alexa, turn down the music!

(Music lowers.)

HARKER. So good to finally be here.

*(***DRACULA** shakes his hand, and **HARKER** shrinks in pain.)*

It was...quite a journey.

---

* A license to produce *DRACULA: A COMEDY OF TERRORS* does not include a performance license for any third-party or copyrighted recordings. Licensees should create their own.

DRACULA. Welcome to my house. Please note that you have entered under no duress and of your own free will.

(Sound effects: Door close – bank vault finality.)

HARKER. Isn't that a unique greeting?

DRACULA. Liability issues.

HARKER. Speaking of, is your solicitor here? For the signing, I mean.

DRACULA. I couldn't find one who keeps my hours.

HARKER. Yes, I *was* wondering why we had to meet so late. It's a bit...unorthodox, isn't it?

DRACULA. I'm a unicorn. You actually caught me in the middle of my morning workout.

HARKER. Morning? It's nearly midnight.

DRACULA. I slept late. *(Pivoting.)* Where are my manners? Can I get you something to drink? To eat?

*(**DRACULA** sexily removes **HARKER**'s jacket.)*

HARKER. You wouldn't happen to have anything gluten free, cruelty free, vegan, non-GMO, and certified organic, would you?

DRACULA. *(To himself.)* I love houseguests.

*(To **HARKER**.)* You're in luck. I get all my overpriced produce from the farmers market in town.

HARKER. Perfect. In fact, that's where my carriage driver got this fresh garlic! Look!

> *(He pulls out the braid of garlic. **DRACULA** recoils, hisses.)*

You alright there, Dracula?

DRACULA. Oh, yes. Just...allergic.

HARKER. Bad luck! Makes cooking a challenge, eh?

DRACULA. Not at all! I'm a baker. More sweet than savory.

HARKER. Oh, lovely. I'm sure Mrs. Dracula appreciates that.

DRACULA. *(Weighted.)* There is no Mrs. Dracula.

(Sound effects: Lonely wolf howl.)

HARKER. Oh. Forgive my presumption.

DRACULA. No, naturally you assumed as much.

(Music in.)*

I'm highly desirable.

*(Snap – **DRACULA** rips off his vest and, bare chested, begins to work out with resistance bands.)*

But I've been through every single person in Romania, and I have yet to find the right one.

HARKER. It is a small country, I suppose.

DRACULA. Full of small-minded people. How many more conversations can a man have about chicken coops and borscht? I long for someone who will *challenge* me; a match; an equal! Someone whose strength of character makes me want to be better.

(Beat.)

Also, they have to be hot. That is what I truly crave, Mr. Harker; the love, the companionship, the *taste* of that one special person.

HARKER. The taste?

DRACULA. I'm sorry, the *trust* of that one special person.

---

*A license to produce *DRACULA: A COMEDY OF TERRORS* does not include a performance license for any third-party or copyrighted recordings. Licensees should create their own.

HARKER. Well, no shortage of singletons in London! Let's get you there straight away. I have all the legal documents for you to take ownership of your five new properties.

DRACULA. Wonderful.

*(They sit next to one another. **HARKER** offers him a thick stack of legal papers to sign.)*

HARKER. So I'll just need your autograph here.

(He offers a pen and points where to sign.)

Here. Here. Here. Here.

DRACULA. I'm not even reading this.

*(**HARKER** flips a page.)*

HARKER. Here. Here. Here. And initial...

(Another page.)

Here. Lovely. And then there's the little matter...of the cheque.

DRACULA. Ah yes, I have that prepared.

*(Sound effects: Chimes. **DRACULA** pulls a cheque out of thin air [sleight of hand].)*

HARKER. *(Salivating.)* Cheers very much. Lots of zeros on this one, eh?

DRACULA. Remarkable. Real estate has gone through the roof since the Punic Wars.

HARKER. *(Laughing too eagerly.)* Punic wars! You're funny! Yes, it's bloody expensive isn't it?

DRACULA. Yes, bloody expensive.

(Sound effects: Rumble.)

HARKER. Count. Not to pry, but I'm curious. What does one do with five separate homes in London?

DRACULA. Investments. I want to have a foothold in all the best neighborhoods.

HARKER. I admire your business acumen. Might I ask what you do for work?

DRACULA. *(Deflecting.)* You Englishmen are all business.

>*(**DRACULA** crosses back to him seductively, admiring his neck.)*

Might *I* ask what *you* do for *pleasure*?

>*(**HARKER** tries to remain upbeat, even as he feels **DRACULA**'s fiery gaze.)*

HARKER. I don't know. Usual things. A tidy desk generally makes me happy. Cup of tea, not too hot. Hand sanitizer, any brand.

DRACULA. You sound like a lot of fun.

HARKER. *(Laughing along.)* Hahahaha...

>*(Then.)*

I'm not. My fiancée tells me all the time. She's much more adventurous than I am.

DRACULA. Is that so?

>*(Woosh! **DRACULA** waves his arm over **HARKER**, who leans forward as **DRACULA**'s leg flies over him. **HARKER** pops back up, unaware.)*

HARKER. Yes, she's always off exploring dark and abandoned places, picking up exotic plants and artifacts and getting herself into all sorts of mischief.

DRACULA. She sounds fearless.

HARKER. She is! I've no idea what she's doing with me.

(Taking out a small framed photograph of her. **DRACULA** *is smitten.)*

Here. This is her. Isn't she a vision?

(Music.)*

DRACULA. She is exquisite.

*(***DRACULA*** *takes the photo and crosses away with it, transfixed.)*

HARKER. Yes, and brave beyond reason. We met as children when I fell through the ice in the pond behind our school, and she rescued me. I would've died of hypothermia had she not heard my screams and come running.

DRACULA. Unbelievable.

HARKER. It's as though she's attracted to danger.

*(***HARKER*** *checks legal papers, stamps them.)*

DRACULA. That neck. The likes of which I have not seen in at least a thousand years.

HARKER. Sorry?

DRACULA. And that skin. Such a flawless neck. She looks like a B Positive, no?

*(***HARKER*** *remains upbeat and engaged but is slightly distracted finishing up his paperwork.)*

HARKER. Oh yes, she's quite the optimist. It's that very spirit which draws people to her.

DRACULA. And her neck.

---

* A license to produce *DRACULA: A COMEDY OF TERRORS* does not include a performance license for any third-party or copyrighted recordings. Licensees should create their own.

(**HARKER** *crosses to* **DRACULA**.)

HARKER. Yes you keep saying that.

DRACULA. Where does she sleep?

HARKER. I'm sorry?

DRACULA. I mean *live*. Where does she live?

HARKER. At her father's house in Whitby, atop a cliff overlooking the North Sea. It's breathtaking.

DRACULA. I like the sound of that.

HARKER. If only her father would give up his silly rehabilitation project with the criminally insane.

DRACULA. Insane?

(**HARKER** *retrieves the framed photo, kisses it and packs up to leave.*)

HARKER. Mental patients who live with him and his daughters.

He specializes in those with weak minds, susceptible to suggestion and vulnerable to dark forces.

DRACULA. Interesting.

HARKER. There's not much else in town, other than the cemetery and Withering Manor.

DRACULA. Withering Manor?

HARKER. A haunted house that no one wants to buy. I've had that listing for ages.

DRACULA. Really? What's the ask?

HARKER. You could pick it up for next to nothing. No one wants to deal with the renovations. Or the screams at night.

DRACULA. I'll take it.

(*Sound effects: Thunder crack.*)

Scene Two

(Sound effects: Fog horn, waves crashing, loud wind.)

*(***ACTOR TWO*** stands on a bench, holding a ship's wheel, **ACTOR ONE** throws on a seaweed-covered poncho. **ACTORS THREE** and **FOUR** hold spray bottles and spritz water into the air toward the scene.)*

CAPTAIN. *(Yelling over the storm.)* Bosun! We're nearing the eye of the storm. Hoist the mizzen and raise the topsail!

BOSUN. *(Irish, yelling over the storm.)* What's that, Captain?

CAPTAIN. I said we're nearing the eye of the storm!

BOSUN. What, I can't hear you!

CAPTAIN. The blasted rain is coming down so hard!

*(***ACTORS THREE*** and **FOUR** spray directly at the **CAPTAIN.**)*

(To **ACTORS.***)* NOT THAT HARD!

*(***ACTORS THREE*** and **FOUR** sheepishly exit.)*

BOSUN. What was that, sir?

CAPTAIN. Never mind! What is the report today?

BOSUN. Due to high winds volleyball has been cancelled.

CAPTAIN. What else?

BOSUN. And...the buffet is down.

CAPTAIN. Damn it.

BOSUN. And you're gonna have to change your own linens, if'n you don't mind, sir.

(The wind picks up and storm rages.)

CAPTAIN. What is this nonsense? We need all hands on deck!

BOSUN. Sir, the men are not well!

(The wind howls.)

CAPTAIN. How's that?

BOSUN. They've all taken ill!

CAPTAIN. How ill?

BOSUN. Dead, sir. Every last one!

CAPTAIN. Every single one?

BOSUN. All but you, me and the passenger. He's been asleep all day. In fact, he's slept every day since we've been on the ship.

(Again, the wind picks up and storm rages.)

CAPTAIN. Then, by God, bring him above. The wind is picking up and we're taking on water. I don't know how much longer she'll hold in this squall.

BOSUN. Aye aye, sir!

(Sound stops. Lights shift.)

CAPTAIN. Captain's log. October 11, 1897. With a trembling hand and a screaming stomach, I attempt to chronicle the terrifying events of the past few days aboard the SS *Stoker*. When the ship left port in the Baltic Sea, she carried thirty-six souls. Since then, however, they've all succumbed to a mysterious illness of the blood, leaving no clue, apart from what appear to be tiny bite marks on their necks. I assume it is somehow related to an aviary disease, as there have been reported sightings of a bat flying from cabin to cabin. The lone passenger below decks has not surfaced in days. I sent our Bosun down to retrieve him, but neither has returned. I can only imagine they have succumbed to the same fate as the rest. I am now left alone at the helm of what is essentially a ghost ship. If I should meet my watery end, please tell my wife and my mistress that she was the only woman I ever loved.

> *(Sound effects: A giant wave grows in front of him.)*

Oh, no. Can that be a wall of water? Here it comes... the big one... I go down honorably with my shiiiiih–

> *(Sound effects: Vacuum sound. Lights shift immediately to:)*

Scene Three

(Whitby, UK; bedroom, Westfeldt house.)

*(***LUCY WESTFELDT***, lovely English rose and would-be adventurer, reads from a wet leather-bound journal, while **MINA WESTFELDT**, her rather awkward sister, picks sand out of her hair.)*

LUCY. I go down honorably with my shih–.

MINA. Lucy, your hair is so lovely. If only I weren't cursed with this ginger monstrosity.

LUCY. Nonsense, Mina, you hair is every bit as beautiful as my own.

MINA. No, you inherited Mother's beauty. All I inherited was flat feet and low self-esteem.

LUCY. Not true! You have great spirit, and you're unafraid to speak your mind.

MINA. I suppose that's why I'm so unlucky in love. Uch, I'll never get all this sand out before the party starts. I hope your little beach expedition was worth it.

LUCY. It was! With all that wreckage washed up, it was like walking right into an adventure story. Feel! This Captain's log is still wet.

MINA. What else does it say? You know I can't read words.

LUCY. I go down honourably with my "shih"

MINA. *(Fascinated.)* With his "shih"?

LUCY. That's where it ends.

MINA. *(Rapt.)* What do you suppose he meant by "going down with his shih"?

LUCY. Oh, sweet sister. I mean...no one survived!

MINA. *(Horrified.)* How chilling! Was there anything else in that book?

LUCY. No. Just some pencil sketches of naked mermaids and the odd cabin boy.

> *(She turns it lengthwise to admire it, as if it's a centerfold.)*

MINA. *(Moved almost to tears.)* Oh, to lose another artist. The world is the poorer for it.

LUCY. Look! There's a manifest here at the end!

MINA. Ooo! That sounds promising.

LUCY. It's all a bit squishy, but this last line looks like it says…six coffins…full of earth…headed for Withering Manor.

MINA. That dreadful abandoned house on the other side of town? Didn't Jonathan just sell that property?

LUCY. Yes, to a man in Transylvania. He must have been on that ship.

MINA. I hope Jonathan cashed the cheque.

> *(**RENFIELD**, a disheveled resident mental patient dressed as a butler in an untied straight jacket, enters.)*

RENFIELD. Pardon me, Miss Lucy. Sorry to bother you, but Mr. Harker's arrived. Shall I send him up?

LUCY. Yes, thank you, Renfield.

MINA. Thank you, Renfield.

LUCY. Incidentally, excellent progress you're making. It seems father's treatments are really working.

RENFIELD. Yes mum. I've gone nearly a week without eating a single insect.

LUCY. Wonderful!

RENFIELD. Oh look, a spider.

MINA. Where?

RENFIELD. On your back!

> (**MINA** *panics, screams, runs around the room, trying to get it off her,* **RENFIELD** *in pursuit, salivating.*)

MINA. Get it off! Get it off!

> (**RENFIELD** *captures the spider and shoves it in his mouth, panting.*)

LUCY. I thought you were working on that.

RENFIELD. *(While eating.)* It's my cheat day.

> (**RENFIELD** *exits.* **HARKER** *enters.*)

HARKER. Is everything alright in here?

MINA. Apologies, Jonathan. My nerves got the better of –

HARKER. Oh thank God, Lucy, you're alright. Almost ready?

LUCY. Of course, darling.

MINA. I'm alright too, thanks.

HARKER. *(Barely acknowledging her.)* Great Mina.

> *(Back to* **LUCY**.*)*

Darling, you're not even dressed! According to my schedule, we're due downstairs in three minutes. How does it look if we're late to our own engagement party?

LUCY. Like our passion is so fiery, we've run off to some far flung land to live on berries and lovemaking. Like in one of those adventure stories. Wouldn't that be something?

HARKER. Something dangerous. Do you know unwashed berries contain parasites? Come on, let's go!

LUCY. I wasn't being literal. I wish you would relax, darling.

HARKER. I'm sorry. I am trying, you know?

LUCY. I know, my love.

(Flirtatiously.) Maybe let's go with*out* a tie tonight.

(She pulls apart his bowtie.)

HARKER. Lucy I had just gotten it perfect!

LUCY. Come on, it's rakish. You look so handsome.

HARKER. Don't poke fun.

LUCY. I'm not! I just want you to loosen up a bit. Give us a kiss.

HARKER. I don't see how that's going to –

*(**LUCY** kisses him.)*

Ooh, that was nice. How about another, future Mrs. Harker?

(They kiss slightly more passionately.)

(Overwhelmed.) We're wicked aren't we? Sorry, Mina.

MINA. It's okay, I like to watch.

HARKER. *(To **LUCY**.)* What's all this sand in your hair?

(He picks it out lovingly.)

LUCY. I was down at the beach last night foraging for souvenirs from the wreck!

HARKER. At night? Are you out of your mind? There are all sorts of ruffians and thugs. They come out of the woodwork whenever a ship runs aground.

LUCY. Jonathan, I appreciate the concern, but there's no need to be skittish.

HARKER. I can't help it. I worry about your safety. A woman shouldn't be out on her own after nightfall.

LUCY. That's silly.

HARKER. It's all a little close to home for my taste. Do you know my incredibly wealthy client Count Dracula was on that ship?

MINA. A Count? Is he single?!

HARKER. Was. Apparently he went down with the ship.

MINA. Will he be at the party?

HARKER. Um, probably not.

MINA. Why do bad things always happen to me?!

HARKER. It's tragic, really. He seemed a nice enough chap. I even invited him to tonight. He was so looking forward to meeting you, Lucy.

MINA. *(Resentful.)* Naturally.

HARKER. He was rather impressed with your skin care regime.

LUCY. Regime? It's just soap and water!

HARKER. Of course, beautiful inside and out. Silver lining, I can sell creepy old Withering Manor again! And all those properties in London. Double commission!

LUCY. How nice!

MINA. Yay, more good things happening for my sister. Meanwhile, I discovered another gray hair down near my –

LUCY. Mina!

MINA. Hmmmm?

LUCY. Will you give us a moment?

MINA. Of course.

(**LUCY** *and* **HARKER** *canoodle on the bed.*
MINA *tries to watch.*)

LUCY. Alone?

MINA. Oh, yes. I'll just head down to the party, then.

LUCY. Wonderful.

MINA. There are quite a few handsome gentlemen. Some
of your former suitors, in fact!

LUCY. Have fun.

MINA. *(Crossing fingers.)* Hoping for sloppy seconds!

LUCY. Mina!

MINA. *(Immediately.)* Going.

(**MINA** *exits,* **HARKER** *notices* **LUCY***'s hair.*)

HARKER. My darling?

MINA. Yes?

HARKER. Is that seaweed?

(*He starts to pluck it out, and she embraces
him.*)

LUCY. Oh, leave it. People will think we've been rolling
around on the beach.

HARKER. It's six degrees and raining. We'd end up in bed
for a week.

LUCY. I would love a week in bed with you, Jonathan.

(*She gets playful with him. He jumps up.*)

HARKER. You're a devil, you are. But we can't do this now!

LUCY. Why not?

HARKER. We have a room full of important guests waiting,
including three judges, a barrister and a beadle.

(**RENFIELD** *pops his head in.*)

RENFIELD. Did someone say beetle?

LUCY & HARKER. No!

(**RENFIELD** *pops his head out.*)

HARKER. Darling, please.

LUCY. *(Disappointed.)* So I guess tonight is for all those important people, then.

HARKER. Lucy, you know you are the most important person in my entire world. You're my future. I love you.

LUCY. And I, you, my darling.

HARKER. In sickness and in health, 'til death do us part.

(Sound effects: Thunder, lightning.)

Scene Four

(In the drawing room of the Westfeldt home.)

(Music.)*

(Lucy and Mina's uptight and sexist father, **DR. WALLACE WESTFELDT**, *presides, with pipe in hand.* **MINA** *stands by demurely with a fan.)*

DR. WESTFELDT. *(Tapping on a glass.)* Ladies and gentlemen, friends and colleagues. For those of you I have yet to meet, I am Dr. Wallace Westfeldt, happy father of the bride and man of the house.

(Holds up a tray of hors d'oeuvres.)

Has everyone had a cheeseball? Prepared just this morning by my staff, who are also my mental patients! But please – they are learning to blend into polite society, so be sure to treat them as poorly as you would anyone else in the service industry! Cheers!

(Sound effects: More applause and approvals. Music resumes.)

MINA. Well done, daddy.

DR. WESTFELDT. Thank you Mina.

MINA. *(Spotting suitors offstage.)* Look who it is, Whitby's most eligible bachelors!

*(**LORD CAVENDISH**, **LORD WORTHINGTON** and **LORD HAVEMERCY** enter. They are, in fact, two puppets held on either side of **ACTOR ONE** who wears a cowboy hat and fake mustache.)*

---

* A license to produce *DRACULA: A COMEDY OF TERRORS* does not include a performance license for any third-party or copyrighted recordings. Licensees should create their own.

DR. WESTFELDT. Capital! Why don't you introduce me?

MINA. Yes, father. This is the very charming Lord Cavendish.

CAVENDISH. *(Scottish accent.)* How do you do?

MINA. And the handsome Lord Worthington.

WORTHINGTON. *(RP British accent.)* Lovely to meet you. Charmed, I'm sure.

MINA. And from America, the ruggedly individual Lord Havemercy.

HAVEMERCY. *(Yosemite Sam.)* Howdy!!

DR. WESTFELDT. Pleasure. Nice to see all this attention being lavished on my daughter.

WORTHINGTON. We prefer your other daughter.

CAVENDISH. Lucy.

HAVEMERCY. The hot one.

MINA. But Lucy is no longer on the market. I, however, am unencumbered by any suitors at all. So if you gentlemen should have even the slightest bit of interest –

DR. WESTFELDT. Alright, alright. Soft touch, darling.

CAVENDISH. And where is your sister?

WORTHINGTON. I'm eager to bestow my well wishes.

MINA. Of course you are.

> **(KITTY RUTHERFORD,** *an elderly kleptomaniac mental patient turned maid, offers them champagne.)*

KITTY. Anyone care for a top off?

DR. WESTFELDT. Kitty, please go fetch Lucy and Jonathan. You can tell the lovebirds they have a restless crowd down here.

KITTY. Yes, Dr. Westfeldt. Anything else I can get ya?

DR. WESTFELDT. You can get me my stethoscope. I noticed it went missing after our last checkup.

KITTY. Yes, mister doctor, sir.

> *(She slowly pulls the stethoscope from her apron pocket.)*

DR. WESTFELDT. I can't very well be expected to cure your kleptomania without the tools of my trade, can I?

KITTY. No, sir doctor mister.

> *(**KITTY** starts to go.)*

DR. WESTFELDT. And also, my watch.

> *(She removes the watch from her apron, sheepishly hands it over.)*

LUCY. How'd that get in there?

> *(As she exits she pilfers the watch from **LORD WORTHINGTON**'s wrist.)*

MINA. I, for one, think Kitty is making excellent progress.

WORTHINGTON. Dr. Westfeldt, do all your patients really live right here in the house with you?

DR. WESTFELDT. Marvelous, isn't it!

CAVENDISH. Are you not concerned about your daughters' safety?

DR. WESTFELDT. Gentlemen, insanity is merely society's failure to recognize individuality and sparkle.

MINA. Father is an advocate for sparkle.

DR. WESTFELDT. I am. I love sparkles. I can't deny it.

WORTHINGTON. But they are dangerous!

MINA. Sparkles?

HAVEMERCY. No, crazy people.

MINA. These people are not *crazy*, they are ill!

> *(Sound effects: Music stops abruptly, party gasps then goes silent.)*

(With genuine passion.) They are suffering. They live a lonely existence, and no one is able to see them for their true worth. They are overlooked, under-acknowledged, and judged by a world obsessed with externals. So if none of you recognize their potential, then none of you are worthy to call yourself my suitor.

HAVEMERCY. We weren't!

MINA. I'm sorry?

HAVEMERCY. No offense, but you're not exactly our type.

WORTHINGTON. But then, you're not anyone's type, are you?

> *(They all laugh at her, building into a nightmarish cacophony.)*

MINA. Vultures! Get out of our house now!

> *(The suitors leave, mumbling their disapprovals.)*

DR. WESTFELDT. Well done, Mina. I didn't know you had that in you.

MINA. *(Overwhelmed.)* Neither did I. There are other things I wish I had in me.

DR. WESTFELDT. *(Coughs.)* Mina.

MINA. But alas, I am destined to live my life unloved and alone.

> *(Sound effects: Woosh.)*

> *(**DRACULA** magically appears in the room, holding a cake.)*

DRACULA. Good evening. Allow me to introduce myself. I am Count Dracula.

*(Music: "Funky Vampire Theme." *)*

(He sprays fog in a can on himself for some extra drama.)

MINA. *(Smitten.)* Hello.

DRACULA. Is this the Westfeldt residence?

DR. WESTFELDT. Indeed. I'm Dr. Westfeldt; Lucy's father. Also, this one.

*(**MINA** giggles and curtsies.)*

MINA. Mina.

(Proudly.) I got all the recessive genes.

DRACULA. Apologies for my tardiness. I'm new in town.

MINA. Count, may I ask you something?

DRACULA. Of course! I'm not afraid to talk about myself.

MINA. Well, isn't that a refreshing quality in a man! Are you...here on your own?

DRACULA. Indeed.

MINA. *(Whispers to heavens.)* Thank you.

DRACULA. Where can I find Lucy?

MINA. Oh, she and Jonathan are canoodling upstairs. Naughty naughty! Not that I'm a prude or anything. Quite the opposite. I've been riding horses for years.

*(She stares into **COUNT DRACULA**'s eyes and makes a horse sound blowing her lips.)*

---

* A license to produce *DRACULA: A COMEDY OF TERRORS* does not include a performance license for any third-party or copyrighted recordings. Licensees should create their own.

DRACULA. Understood. I baked this for the happy couple. It's a Babka.

DR. WESTFELDT. Oh, unfortunately Jonathan has a few dietary –

DRACULA. I know. It's gluten free, cruelty free, vegan, non-GMO, and certified organic. I also brought one for the rest of us that tastes good.

(They takes pieces and eat.)

DR. WESTFELDT. Lovely jubbly.

MINA. Oh. My. God. You're amazing, aren't you?

DRACULA. I do my best. I used extra salt. Good for blood pressure.

DR. WESTFELDT. Wouldn't that *raise* the blood pressure?

DRACULA. To balance the sweet. Marie Antoinette's chef gave me that tip before he lost his head.

DR. WESTFELDT. *(A beat, then laughing.)* Oh, he's having us on. We're going to have to watch out for you! I'll just have Kitty plate this for the guests.

*(He exits. **DRACULA** removes his cape.)*

MINA. Marie Antoinette? How old *are* you?

(Sound effects: Wolves howl.)

DRACULA. Old enough to appreciate beauty found in the most unexpected of places.

*(He hands **MINA** his cape, their hands touch.)*

MINA. *(Blushing, giggly.)* Oh, sir. Your hand is so smooth.

DRACULA. You like that? The secret is staying out of the sun.

*(She giggles. **DR. WESTFELDT** re-enters with **LUCY** and **HARKER**, tapping a spoon on a champagne glass to get everyone's attention.)*

DR. WESTFELDT. Mina, come join us.

> *(She joins her father and sister up front for the speech.)*

Ladies and gentlemen, I give you...the bride and groom-to-be... my lovely daughter Lucy Westfeldt and her intended, Jonathan Harker.

> *(Sound effects: Applause all around.)*

How about a toast, then, Jonathan?

HARKER. No thanks. I'm hopeless with public speaking.

DR. WESTFELDT. Oh come now, it's your engagement party! Say something!

> *(**HARKER** smiles, cowers.)*

LUCY. Father?

DR. WESTFELDT. Hmmm?

LUCY. It's also *my* engagement party.

DR. WESTFELDT. Oh, quite right.

> *(He gives her the floor.)*

LUCY. Thank you.

(To audience.) And thank *you* – for being here tonight to celebrate with us. It's funny.

Jonathan and I have known each other so long we sometimes forget we aren't already married. He's been a constant fixture in this house since we were children. My mother always joked that we would marry one day, and now here we are. How about that. I only wish she could be here to see it. But I know she is smiling down on us now.

> *(**MINA** gets misty. **LUCY** grabs her hand.)*

It's alright sister, I've got you. Cheers, everyone.

(Sound effects: Polite applause.)

DR. WESTFELDT. Yes, drink up! And if anyone is interested in my *other* daughter, Mina. All offers will be considered.

(Sound effects: Confused slow applause.)

*(**MINA** looks toward where the one applauder was, pointing toward them with desperate hope. **DR. WESTFELDT** pulls her away.)*

Come, darling. Let's greet our guests.

*(**DR. WESTFELDT**, **LUCY** and **MINA** exit to talk to other "guests.")*

DRACULA. Jonathan!

HARKER. I don't believe my eyes! Dracula, old man! You're alive!

*(**DRACULA** hoists him into the air.)*

DRACULA. I wouldn't go that far.

HARKER. But I thought everyone on that ship perished!

DRACULA. I managed a narrow escape.

HARKER. Extraordinary! We must let the papers know.

*(**DRACULA** dips him for a beat.)*

DRACULA. No, please. It was harrowing enough to live through once.

HARKER. Yes, of course. But the story! It's tremendous. You'd be famous.

DRACULA. Ehhh. I'm happy living in the shadows.

HARKER. Well, I'm so very glad to see you. And looking rather well, all things considered.

DRACULA. You don't think I need a haircut? Maybe a little off the top?

HARKER. There's a mirror over there if you want to take a look.

DRACULA. Mirrors aren't really my thing.

(**LUCY, MINA** *and* **DR. WESTFELDT** *approach.*)

LUCY. Jonathan, darling, your friends are absolute charmers.

HARKER. You haven't met them all. We've a late arrival.

DRACULA. Lucy! Your fiancée has told me so much about you.

LUCY. Has he? All good I hope.

HARKER. Naturally.

DRACULA. Count Dracula. You are even more compelling in person.

(*He kneels and kisses her hand too long.*)

LUCY. Thanks. I don't believe anyone has ever…"french kissed" my hand before. How…Continental.

DR. WESTFELDT. Count, where did you say you were from?

DRACULA. The Carpathian mountains.

HARKER. The Count just purchased Withering Manor.

DR. WESTFELDT. Really? Bit of a fixer upper, eh?

DRACULA. It's perfect as is.

DR. WESTFELDT. Even with the mold? And the bugs? And the smell?

DRACULA. I'm used to it. I have a time-share in Florida.

HARKER. This is a highly resilient man. He's the sole survivor of last night's ship wreck!

DR. WESTFELDT. Really? You certainly clean up well.

LUCY. Count, the ship's manifest reported six boxes of soil from abroad. You wouldn't know anything about that would you?

DRACULA. As a matter of fact, they are mine. I plan to grow some of my native herbs from back home. For baking.

LUCY. Fascinating.

DRACULA. Yes, baking appeals to the sensuality of my soul.

> (*As he speaks,* **MINA** *gets increasingly turned on.*)

Working the supple dough, watching it slowly rise and give off heat, then feeding it to my lover as their eyes roll backwards and they moan and beg for more.

> (*Thunk!* **MINA** *drops to the bench. Uncomfortable beat.*)

LUCY. I actually meant the *soil* was fascinating.

DRACULA. Oh, that's just dirt.

LUCY. (*Passionately.*) Just dirt? Every handful of earth contains an entire world of minerals, gases, liquids. All the things that give us life!

DRACULA. Wow.

LUCY. I'm sorry I do get carried away. I was an earth sciences major at Oxford.

DRACULA. Oxford? Impressive.

LUCY. Not really. It wasn't like I came in top of my class and then couldn't find work because I was a woman. Oh, wait.

DR. WESTFELDT. Bright side is – she's about to start the most important job of all – wife and mother!

LUCY. (*Unconvincing.*) Yay.

DRACULA. Lucy, might I invite you over to see my soil samples?

LUCY. That's very generous of you, Count.

DRACULA. Excellent. Come with me now.

LUCY. Now? In the middle of my engagement party? Silly. We'll find time in the next week or two.

DRACULA. Oh. So you don't want to –

LUCY. Go home with you?

(She laughs. They all join in, assuming **DRACULA** *is making a joke.)*

DRACULA. I usually don't have to ask twice.

(They all continue laughing. **DRACULA** *joins in for a moment, trying to play along, then:)*

I'm serious.

LUCY. Thanks for the laugh, Count. Welcome to Whitby.

HARKER. Come Lucy, darling. I want to introduce you to my cousins, Mary and Shelly.

(Sound effects: Musical flourish.)*

*(***MINA** *and* **DR. WESTFELDT** *approach.)*

MINA. Raise your hand if you're awkward at parties!

*(***MINA** *raises her hand. No one else does.)*

Just me? Soooo how are you getting on? Has Renfield offered you a canapé?

DRACULA. Renfield?

---

*A license to produce *DRACULA: A COMEDY OF TERRORS* does not include a performance license for any third-party or copyrighted recordings. Licensees should create their own.

DR. WESTFELDT. One of my patients. And my butler. He's working the party to develop his social skills.

       (**DR. WESTFELDT** *calls offstage to* **RENFIELD.**)

Renfield!

       (**ACTOR TWO** *leans behind proscenium [or faces upstage] to respond as* **RENFIELD** *and back out [or downstage] to respond as* **DR. WESTFELDT.**)

RENFIELD. *(Offstage.)* Yes, doctor!

DR. WESTFELDT. Will you please come back in here?

RENFIELD. *(Offstage.)* Coming, doctor!

DR. WESTFELDT. He's got little to no confidence, so he's highly suggestible.

DRACULA. Is that so?

MINA. *(Confidential.)* And he eats bugs.

DR. WESTFELDT. I'll see what's keeping him. Renfield!

       (**DR. WESTFELDT** *exits.*)

MINA. *(Awkwardly.)* Seems it's just the two of us here for the moment. I've always preferred to socialize in smaller groups. Large tables of gossiping girls always make me somewhat anxious so this a rare treat.

DRACULA. Indeed.

MINA. I like your trousers.

DRACULA. Thank you.

MINA. And your shirt.

DRACULA. Thanks.

MINA. And your...face.

       (**DR. WESTFELDT** *calls from offstage.*)

DR. WESTFELDT. *(Offstage.)* Mina!

MINA. *(Petulant teenager.)* DAD, I'M COMING! GOD!

(To **DRACULA**.*)* You must be parched from your shipwreck. I'll get you a drink.

> *(***MINA*** exits. ***ACTOR TWO*** re-enters as* ***RENFIELD**.)*

RENFIELD. Good evening, sir. Would you like a cheesy fing?

*(***DRACULA*** identifies his next target.)*

DRACULA. Let me guess… Renfield.

RENFIELD. Do I know you?

DRACULA. Not yet. But I know *you.*

RENFIELD. You do?

DRACULA. Better than you know yourself. You're lonely. You're misunderstood. You're without purpose.

RENFIELD. It's like you can see right into my soul. My only relief is in serving others.

(A big turn on for **DRACULA**.*)*

DRACULA. Well, I've got a little penchant for being served. And I could use some help cleaning up around Withering Manor in case I should have a guest. You're not afraid of a *bug* or two, are you?

RENFIELD. *(Salivating.)* Bugs?! What kind of bugs?! Can you be more specific?

DRACULA. Why don't you come by later tonight and see for yourself? I'll prepare an assortment. When it comes to living ingredients, I'm a master chef.

RENFIELD. *(Excited.)* A master chef?!

DRACULA. Come by. Three a.m. Tell no one.

RENFIELD. Yes, Master –

    (Sound effects: Thunder, lightning.)

Chef.

    *(He leaves. **MINA** returns with two drinks.)*

    (Romantic violin music.)*

MINA. *(Flirtatious, liquid courage.)* I'm back! Who's thirsty?! Down the hatch!

    (She downs her drink, he abstains.)

Count, might I be so bold as to ask...for a dance?

DRACULA. I wish I could, but I'm famished. I have to go find someone, *something,* to eat.

MINA. Oh, I'd be happy to fix you a plate.

DRACULA. No thanks, I'm on a special...liquid diet.

MINA. Just a quick spin, then?

DRACULA. A quick one; but full disclosure, I'm not emotionally available. My heart lies elsewhere.

MINA. *(Earnestly.)* And my heart is so very hungry, that even your table scraps will feel like a banquet.

DRACULA. Very well, then.

    (They bow and dance, slowly.)

MINA. You're much livelier than my usual dance partner.

DRACULA. And who is that?

MINA. The bench over there.

DRACULA. Has anyone ever told you, you have beautiful veins?

---

* A license to produce *DRACULA: A COMEDY OF TERRORS* does not include a performance license for any third-party or copyrighted recordings. Licensees should create their own.

MINA. *(Giggling.)* Why, no! No, they haven't. They usually comment on my thick fingers or extra tooth.

*(She beams. **DRACULA** coughs.)*

DRACULA. I was...talking about the varicose veins in your neck.

MINA. My neck! What a refreshing compliment.

DRACULA. The way it curves gently, pitching it at just the right angle to show off your exquisite jugular.

MINA. You're not like all the other men in Whitby, are you?

DRACULA. Transylvania is very far from here. Simply put, I'm a stranger in a strange land.

MINA. *(Melting to him.)* Funny. I've always felt that way myself.

DRACULA. Of course you have. All of us are alone, aren't we? Craving momentary comfort in the arms of one who will hold you tight, caress your face, and take complete control of you.

(**MINA** *drops all pretense of daintiness, desperate for him.*)

MINA. *(Gutteral.)* You wanna get outta here?

DRACULA. My house is just across town.

MINA. Good. I'll grab a bottle.

DRACULA. Don't bother. I'm thirsty for something else.

(Sound effects: Thunder, lightning.)

Scene Five

DR. WESTFELDT. 15 October, 1897. To Doctor Jean *(Pronounced Jhhhon.)* Van Helsing, University of *Schmutz*, Brandenburg Campus, Department of Rare Infectious Diseases. Dear Doctor Van Helsing. I write to you now in dire need of your expertise. Three days ago, my eldest daughter Mina was at her sister's engagement party, with a ruddy complexion and full of life. The following morning, we found her bedridden and pale, her veins swollen with an odd colour, and unable to look at direct sunlight without wincing in pain. At first I assumed it was a female issue, but it's even more frightening than that. I cannot pinpoint the source of her distress. I beg of you to come see us straight away. Speaking man to man, I fear for her life.

(Music in.)*

(Mina's sickbed faces upstage, so we only see the back of the headboard with her ginger hair cascading over the top of it. **LUCY** *ministers to her, while* **HARKER** *keeps his distance, a handkerchief close to his mouth.)*

LUCY. Oh, my dear sweet Mina. How it pains me to see her like this. Look at her face, Jonathan. She looks haggard and sickly.

(He observes from a distance.)

HARKER. Looks the same to me.

LUCY. Because you're standing on the other side of the room. Come closer, look at her veins. It's as if her blood is boiling.

---

* A license to produce *DRACULA: A COMEDY OF TERRORS* does not include a performance license for any third-party or copyrighted recordings. Licensees should create their own.

HARKER. Oh yes, very troubling. Why don't I pop downstairs? Give you your privacy, yes? Might be a good time for me to work on the menu for the wedding?

LUCY. Jonathan! If my sister does not improve, there will be no wedding.

HARKER. Of course.

LUCY. I pray Dr. Van Helsing is able to help. Renfield is picking him up at the station now.

(**MINA** *lets out a moan of pain.****)

Mina! Sweet sister! Are you in pain?

(**MINA** *lets out another moan.*)

HARKER. Sounds like a no to me!

(**MINA** *moans louder.*)

Or a yes. I'll go see if Renfield is back with the doctor.

(*He runs out.* **MINA** *moans.*)

LUCY. There, there, sister. Do not be afraid. Whatever this terrible illness is that has befallen you, you will beat it. You will! You hear me? But you must be strong!

Remember what mother told us when we were children?

That night when the tempest from the sea made that horrible howling against our bedroom window, and you were convinced there was someone coming for us? She would not let us hide under the covers. She walked us to the window, opened it wide, and let the air in to prove there was nothing outside that could hurt us... apart from the serial killer that murdered the family next door. But mother's advice still holds! Whatever this is *will pass*, but you must fight! For the sake of

---

* **MINA**'s moans should be either pre-recorded or performed by **ACTOR FOUR** from offstage.

your family; for the sake of your future; for the sake of
the medical students who study you every spring.

(**HARKER** *re-enters.*)

HARKER. No sign of the doctor. I must say, it's highly
unnerving to see a person so lively and gay one moment
and then down for the count the next.

LUCY. *(Light bulb.)* The Count! Count Dracula!

HARKER. What about him?

LUCY. My God, why didn't I think of that?

HARKER. Think of what?

LUCY. His cake! He must've used spoiled ingredients from
Transylvania. It's just food poisoning!

HARKER. But everyone at the party ate it, including you.
No one else fell ill.

LUCY. Damnit! You're right. It's clearly more acute than that.

(Sound effects: Rumble.)

(**DR. WESTFELDT** *enters, reading charts.*)

DR. WESTFELDT. Just finished testing her blood, she's
severely anemic. We're going to need to start transfusions.

LUCY. I'm happy to donate as much as she needs.

DR. WESTFELDT. Van Helsing will guide us. He's the most
accomplished doctor in all of Germany. There's nothing
he hasn't seen.

(Sound effects: Doorbell chimes.)

Ah, speak of the devil. That'll be him now!

LUCY. Thank goodness. You hear that Mina? You're on
your way to recovery, now that Dr. Van Helsing is here.
And he came all the way from the Continent! Isn't that
something?

(**DR. VAN HELSING,** *a woman in her forties with handsome face, sturdy comportment, and double-braided Bavarian buns on her head, enters. It's the same performer who plays* **MINA.**)

VAN HELSING. Excuse me, Doctor Westfeldt?

DR. WESTFELDT. Hello there! So nice to meet you. You must be...*Mrs.* Van Helsing?

VAN HELSING. *Doctor* Van Helsing.

DR. WESTFELDT. Yes, Doctor Van Helsing's *wife.* Is your husband lifting the heavy bags from the carriage?

VAN HELSING. I have no husband.

(*Beat. He starts laughing again.*)

LUCY. Father!

DR. WESTFELDT. Ah, that famous German sense of humor! I'll go help him with the bags.

(*He leaves.*)

LUCY. Apologies, Doctor. My father is under a great deal of stress with my sister's illness. Could you please take a look at her right now? Time is of the essence.

(**VAN HELSING** *approaches the bed, looking under the covers.*)

VAN HELSING. She looks depleted. Any other symptoms?

LUCY. (*Taking stock.*) She complains of terrible dreams, some...sexier than others, and a weakness, a bloodlessness, that confounds her doctors.

VAN HELSING. How long have these bite marks been visible?

HARKER. Bite marks?

VAN HELSING. Right where her carotid artery and jugular intersect.

>(**RENFIELD** *pops his head in from proscenium [We only see his head].*)

RENFIELD. Did someone say insects?

HARKER & LUCY. No!

>(**RENFIELD** *pops his head out [***ACTOR TWO*** removes wig].*)

LUCY. Where's my father.

>(**ACTOR TWO** *immediately re-enters as…*)

DR. WESTFELDT. I'll be damned, the carriage has gone.

VAN HELSING. Peculiar butler you have.

HARKER. He's also a patient.

DR. WESTFELDT. We're wasting precious time. Where is Dr. Van Helsing?

VAN HELSING. I am here.

DR. WESTFELDT. No, you're not! I sent for Doctor Jean [Jhhhon] Van Helsing. As in, Jean [Jhhhon] Valjean [Val-Jhhhon].

VAN HELSING. No, you sent for Doctor Jean [Gene] Van Helsing. As in Jean [Gene] Val-Gene.

DR. WESTFELDT. So I sent for…a lady doctor?

VAN HELSING. Correct.

DR. WESTFELDT. *(Scoffing.)* Ha!

VAN HELSING. I wouldn't schcoff if I were you. Your daughter is in grave danger. This is no ordinary insect bite.

DR. WESTFELDT. What do you mean?

VAN HELSING. It appears she may have been bitten...by something more sinister.

(Sound effects: Musical sting. Wolves howl.)

(Interrogating.) Have any of you been out of the country?

HARKER. I was in Eastern Europe.

VAN HELSING. Did you bring back any fruits or vegetables?

HARKER. *(Pulls out the bag of garlic.)* Just this garlic from the farmers market in Bucharest. But she wasn't exposed to it.

VAN HELSING. Anything else? Maybe something from Duty Free?

HARKER. No.

VAN HELSING. *(Dead serious.)* Good. The savings are minimal. Have you noticed anything or anyone unusual in the area lately?

HARKER. Just the regular, workaday English life. Soggy sandwiches, lots of rain, ghost ship washed up on shore. Nothing out of the ordinary.

VAN HELSING. Hold on. What was that?

HARKER. Nothing out of the ordinary.

VAN HELSING. No, go back a word or two.

HARKER. Shore. On. Up. Washed?

VAN HELSING. Continue –

HARKER. Ship. Ghost?

VAN HELSING. A ghost ship! The very thing. Was there a manifest?

LUCY. Yes! I found it on the beach. There was no cargo at all, apart from some bird seed, canned tuna, and six coffins of Transylvanian earth. Nothing out of the ordinary.

VAN HELSING. Hold on. What was that?

LUCY. Nothing out of the ordinary.

VAN HELSING. No, go back a word or two.

LUCY. Earth. Transylvanian. Of?

VAN HELSING. Continue –

LUCY. Coffins. Six?

VAN HELSING. Six coffins! That could be the key.

DR. WESTFELDT. They key to what, the makeup counter at Selfridge's? This female medicine is not for me, I'm afraid. I'm going out to pick up some leeches and tape worms to drain her evil humours. *Like a real doctor.* I'll be back before nightfall.

(**DR. WESTFELDT** *exits.*)

VAN HELSING. Lucy, I must know, was your sister alone with anyone the night of the party?

LUCY. She attempted to make conversation with three of my former suitors, but I do not believe she left with any one of them.

(**RENFIELD** *laughs as he enters.*)

Renfield! You gave me a fright!

RENFIELD. Words, words, words, words. I can't stop laughing!

HARKER. Now hold it right there. What's funny about a dying girl?

RENFIELD. A dying girl who flirted with *four* gentlemen.

LUCY. But there were only *three*, Renfield.

RENFIELD. There was a fourth. And she left with him that night.

(Suddenly, a bat flies in through the window. **HARKER** *grabs a bat puppet attached to a wire, pretending to run from it and passing it from actor to actor, until it "flies" to* **RENFIELD**, *who wields it as if being attacked.* **LUCY** *grabs a broom.)*

I didn't tell, master, I didn't tell! I'm sorry.

*(***LUCY*** *swings the broom toward the bat, as* **RENFIELD** *leaps behind the headboard with the bat puppet.* **LUCY** *raises the broom on the other side, which has a bat attached to it. She tries to shake it off.)*

VAN HELSING. Why are you speaking to that fluttermouse?

HARKER. It's a bat, doctor.

RENFIELD. It's the devil is what it is.

*(***LUCY*** *swings the broom behind the headboard and brings it back up on the bat-less side as* **RENFIELD** *raises the bat.)*

VAN HELSING. That garlic, do you mind if I have a go with it?

HARKER. Right-o.

VAN HELSING. Danke schoen.

*(***HARKER*** *hands it to her. She raises it in the air toward* **RENFIELD**. *The bat chases* **RENFIELD** *toward the window.)*

RENFIELD. Get that away from him.

VAN HELSING. Him?

RENFIELD. I've already said too much. I'm sorry, master! Ahhhh!

*(He dives out the window, screaming "Ahhhh." **LUCY** runs to the window, joined by **HARKER** and **VAN HELSING** – who all "follow" **RENFIELD**'s very long fall. The "Ahhhh" continues as **ACTOR TWO** quick changes and re-enters as **DR. WESTFELDT**, still holding the "Ah," which becomes...)*

DR. WESTFELDT. Ahhhh – I thought I heard a scream. What happened?

LUCY. What a palaver! It's Renfield! He's gone.

HARKER. Out the window and over the balcony.

VAN HELSING. After conversing with a fluttermouse.

DR. WESTFELDT. Oh, no. And he was doing so well.

HARKER. I wouldn't go that far.

DR. WESTFELDT. He's escaped before. We'll find him.

*(**DR. VAN HELSING** breathes in the air around her.)*

VAN HELSING. You may not want to find him. From the looks of it, he may be the one responsible for your daughter's illness.

DR. WESTFELDT. Do you really think so? He's never hurt so much as a fly.

(Then.)

Oh yeah.

VAN HELSING. Ja. Exactly. There's something foul in the air here.

LUCY. What is happening to us, Doctor?

VAN HELSING. From all the evidence, it can only be one thing.

(Sound effects: Thunder, lightning.)

Scene Six

VAN HELSING. 20th October, 1897. The patient, Mina Westfeldt, grows worse by the hour, with intermittent bouts of extreme aggression. We have been forced to chain her to the bed for her own safety. Our next course of action is to administer blood transfusions. I have only ever read about vampires in ancient medical texts. I assumed they were the schtuff of fiction und fairytales. However, I fear I am about to be proven wrong. If so – Gott help us all.

> *(Music in.*)*

> *(Mina's bedside, the following evening.)*

> *(**LUCY** at Mina's bedside – **HARKER** on the other side of the room.)*

How is she doing? Any improvement this evening?

LUCY. I'm afraid not. The fits are getting worse.

VAN HELSING. Scheisse! I thought the transfusions were working.

LUCY. What's our next course of action, doctor?

VAN HELSING. I will assess!

> *(**VAN HELSING** speaks to Mina, over the headboard.)*

Mina? This is Dr. Van Helsing. Can you hear me?

LUCY. She can hardly speak, doctor. Her lungs are very weak.

> *(**VAN HELSING** leans behind the headboard to hear better – and voices **MINA**.)*

---

*A license to produce *DRACULA: A COMEDY OF TERRORS* does not include a performance license for any third-party or copyrighted recordings. Licensees should create their own.

MINA. *(Sickly.)* Yesss, I can hear you.

> (**VAN HELSING** *comes up from behind headboard.)*

VAN HELSING. Excellent. What a pretty voice you have!

> (**VAN HELSING** *leans behind the headboard to hear better – and voices* **MINA.***)*

MINA. *(Giggling.) He* said I had a pretty *neck.*

> (**VAN HELSING** *comes up from behind headboard.)*

VAN HELSING. Who said you had a pretty neck?

LUCY. She's hallucinating doctor. Clearly no one would ever say that to *her.*

VAN HELSING. Who was it that complimented your neck?

> *(Nightmare music.*)*

> (**VAN HELSING** *and* **LUCY** *pull out stuffed puppet arms with big rubber hands from behind the headboard that they clutch to their necks, as if being strangled.)*

LUCY. Another episode.

VAN HELSING. The chains will hold her.

HARKER. Are you sure?

> (**VAN HELSING** *and* **LUCY** *are pulled into bed behind headboard by "Mina.")*

MINA. Blood! Blood! I must have blood!

---

* A license to produce *DRACULA: A COMEDY OF TERRORS* does not include a performance license for any third-party or copyrighted recordings. Licensees should create their own.

> (**VAN HELSING** *and* **LUCY** *are thrown back out by "Mina."*)

LUCY. Jonathan, quick, grab her feet.

HARKER. You don't think she's contagious, do you?

LUCY. Really, Jonathan, is that the first thought on your mind?

> (**VAN HELSING** *and* **LUCY** *are thrown upstage by "Mina." Then her "grasp" loosens and they settle with a sigh.*)

HARKER. She's surprisingly flexible.

VAN HELSING. It's subsided.

> (**VAN HELSING** *leans behind headboard to fix Mina's blanket.*)

Rest, Mina, rest.

> (*Immediately* **MINA** *falls back asleep. Snores loudly.* **VAN HELSING** *pops back up.*)

She's asleep. You too, my darlings. We all need rest if we are to care for her. Gute nacht, lieblings.

> (**VAN HELSING** *exits.*)

LUCY. Jonathan, will you wipe her forehead?

HARKER. Um... I'm okay, thanks.

LUCY. Would you rather change her bedpan?

HARKER. I'd rather do neither, thank you very much.

LUCY. Jonathan!

HARKER. Germs.

LUCY. She needs us. She is gravely ill.

HARKER. Which is why I'd prefer to stay at a comfortable distance.

LUCY. And if I were to become ill? Would you likewise remain at a comfortable distance from me?

HARKER. Never!

(*Beat.*)

Unless it was communicable.

LUCY. Jonathan!

HARKER. I'm trying! You don't know what it feels like to be inside my skin. This isn't easy for me.

LUCY. Nor is it easy for me living with all your "feelings." There are two of us in this relationship. And we've each got to give a little.

HARKER. I gave you a beautiful necklace for your last birthday!

LUCY. I mean you have to be willing to venture past your fears, go off-piste for once in your life!

HARKER. I want to.

LUCY. Then stop being so frightened of things that might be and start living in the present.

HARKER. Of course I want to live in the present, and I will...very soon!

LUCY. Jonathan! What if I cannot wait any longer? What if I do not wish to negotiate every decision until I'm blue in the face? What if, just once, I want to move through life without fear, with a courageous partner rather than a coward.

(*Beat. They share a look.*)

I didn't mean –

HARKER. Yes you did.

LUCY. Jonathan, please –

HARKER. No. If that's what you want, then you should have it. And not with a tuppenny coward.

> (**HARKER** *exits.*)

LUCY. Jonathan, wait!

> (*Sound effects: Gust of wind.* **DRACULA** *appears magically.*)

DRACULA. (*Urgently.*) How is she holding up?

LUCY. Count! You frightened me. Where did you come from?

DRACULA. I'm here to help. What can I do?

LUCY. I've got it covered for now, but I can't tell you how much it means to me that you offered.

DRACULA. My heart is breaking for you and your family.

LUCY. Thank you. She's got a strong spirit. She'll pull through.

DRACULA. But if she doesn't...

LUCY. She will.

DRACULA. But if she doesn't, her death will not have been in vain.

LUCY. I don't know how people view death where you come from, but in England it is nothing short of a tragedy when it comes so early to a beautiful young girl.

DRACULA. Are we still talking about Mina?

LUCY. Yes of course!

DRACULA. Of course, yes! Also, I'd like to pick up my cake plate, if you don't mind. It's Wedgwood.

LUCY. Yes I'm sorry, I'm just a little unnerved right now. Jonathan and I –

DRACULA. I heard.

LUCY. How did you –

DRACULA. You are a strong courageous woman.

> *(Crawling over* **MINA** *to get to* **LUCY.***)*

You deserve a strong –

MINA. Oof!*

DRACULA. *(Quickly to* **MINA.***)* Sorry.

> *(Back to* **LUCY.***)* – courageous man.

> *(Music.*** **DRACULA** *draws closer to her.)*

LUCY. What are you doing?

DRACULA. Offering you a gift.

> *(He hands her a strange and exotic flower.)*

LUCY. It looks like. No, it couldn't be. Is this a... a Germanicus Vita Vamperious?

DRACULA. It is indeed.

LUCY. I studied them at Oxford. The books say they're extinct.

DRACULA. And yet here it is. Take comfort knowing there is more to life than that which we see in the light of day.

LUCY. I thought it might be a sundew or a waterwheel, but this is clearly carnivorous.

---

* **MINA**'s line should be either pre-recorded or performed by **ACTOR FOUR** from offstage.
** A license to produce *DRACULA: A COMEDY OF TERRORS* does not include a performance license for any third-party or copyrighted recordings. Licensees should create their own.

(Sound effects: Chomp! The flower snaps closed, making **LUCY***'s finger bleed.)*

Ooof! Will you look at that? I'm bleeding.

(She holds her finger up to him, then looks at it, then looks from afar, while **DRACULA** *follows the bloody finger.)*

(Excited.) Isn't that something?

DRACULA. *(Salivating.)* Something delicious.

(He moves in on her, thirsty for her blood.)

LUCY. What was that?

DRACULA. *(Covering.)* Auspicious. Something auspicious: I happen to have a handkerchief.

(He hands it to her, she wipes her finger on it.)

LUCY. Thank you so much. I'll have this washed and ironed and return it to you next week.

DRACULA. Don't you dare! I mean, I wouldn't hear of it. I'll just take that back from you.

LUCY. No, please. It's no problem.

DRACULA. Really, I insist.

LUCY. But aren't you worried about the germs –?

DRACULA. Give it here! Now!

(He jerks it out of her hand, lunges to the ground inhaling it, in need of a fix.)

LUCY. Where did *that* come from?

DRACULA. You inspire it in me. Lucy – fate has dealt me a torturous hand. Being near you only reminds me of what I don't have.

LUCY. You have everything.

DRACULA. Everything except...the one.

> *(Sound effects: Wolf howl. Music.*)*

You don't know what it is to be alone. From the time I was a child, I had to endure the scorn and ridicule of the other children in my village. I couldn't swing a cricket bat if my life depended on it. Also, they had never seen a boy in a cape. They bullied me; stormed my house with torches and horrible epithets. But I got my revenge.

LUCY. How's that?

DRACULA. By becoming very good looking. Also rich. And immortal. That's pretty major.

LUCY. Did you say –

DRACULA. But you can only drink and shop and sleep around for so long until it begins to feel like you've eaten too much dessert and you're rotting inside.

LUCY. I never thought of it that way.

DRACULA. But being here with you, I feel like I'm eating healthy for the first time. You nourish me.

LUCY. Yes, I rather enjoy talking to someone who's not afraid to get his hands dirty, so to speak.

DRACULA. Help me, Lucy. Help me cultivate my garden, and myself. Help me heal. Share your passion, your strength, your fire. And this is something I've never said to anyone before in my life. *Tell me more about you.*

LUCY. Me? Well, I guess I've always wondered why –

DRACULA. Because the more I think about it, the more I feel I've known you forever. I mean, it's so easy to talk

---

* A license to produce *DRACULA: A COMEDY OF TERRORS* does not include a performance license for any third-party or copyrighted recordings. Licensees should create their own.

to you. The conversation just seems to flow without any awkward silences or pauses.

LUCY. Count –

DRACULA. You know what? Come back to Withering Manor, I have so much show you.

(He puts his cape back on, ready to leave.)

LUCY. I would, but my sister –

DRACULA. She's in good hands, trust me.

LUCY. You know Dr. Van Helsing?

DRACULA. I'm intoxicated by you Lucy, distracted beyond reason.

(He moves in on her. She stops him.)

LUCY. Count, please. Your plant is beautiful, but I must remain here to care for Mina.

(He withdraws.)

DRACULA. Forgive me. I am in no rush. For me, time is more of a construct.

LUCY. Thank you.

(She sits on the bed.)

I must be lightheaded from all the transfusions.

DRACULA. Transfusions?

LUCY. Yes, I've given her several pints of blood today and haven't had anything to eat.

*(**DRACULA**'s ears perk up. Lucy's blood?!)*

DRACULA. Lucy, how can you be there for your sister if you do not care for yourself first? Why don't you go make yourself a nice cup of tea?

LUCY. You're right. I could do with some sustenance. Will you watch her for a moment?

DRACULA. My pleasure. And, if you don't mind… the cake plate.

LUCY. *(Dead serious.)* Of course.

>*(She exits.)*

DRACULA. Mina…

>*(Music.* **DRACULA** *jumps on the bed, as if straddling Mina – speaking to the upstage side of the headboard.)*

If I can't taste Lucy's blood from the source, I can now drink it from you!

>*(Sound effects: Thunder.)*

It will soon be time to join the ranks of the undead at Withering Manor. We fly tonight under the cover of darkness, but first show me your neck.

>*(He leans in behind headboard and bites. Music sting. He pops back up with fangs exposed, opening his mouth wide as blood drips from his mouth.)*

>*(Sound effects: Terrifying high-pitched screams of a colony of bats.)*

>**(RENFIELD** *enters, through the window, now covered in mud, ash and tattered clothing.)*

RENFIELD. You called, master?

DRACULA. Your indiscretion almost cost us everything.

---

* A license to produce *DRACULA: A COMEDY OF TERRORS* does not include a performance license for any third-party or copyrighted recordings. Licensees should create their own.

(Woosh! **DRACULA** *extends his hand toward* **RENFIELD** *and controls him physically.)*

RENFIELD. I'm sorry, I am weak! What can I do?

DRACULA. Wait here for Lucy. She will not come with me willingly, so I am taking her blood – in the body of her sister. But not a word, not a whisper, you understand?

RENFIELD. Yes, master.

DRACULA. Good, I don't want to be interrupted. I'm taking my dinner to-go!

(Sound effects: Thunder! **DRACULA** *grabs a mess of blankets with a replica of Mina's wig and jumps out the window.* **RENFIELD** *plays with the drops of Mina's blood left upstage of the headboard.)*

RENFIELD. *(Sings.)*
TWINKLE TWINKLE LITTLE STAR
HOW I WONDER WHAT YOU –

*(***LUCY** *enters with the cake plate.)*

LUCY. I'm sorry, Count, I – Renfield!

RENFIELD. Miss Lucy!

(He shows his bloody hands.)

LUCY. What have you done?

*(***RENFIELD** *giggles.)*

RENFIELD. I'll never tell. I have a secret.

*(***LUCY** *goes to pull the blanket back, revealing an empty bed.)*

LUCY. Where is she?! Answer me!!

RENFIELD. Sorry. Gotta fly!

> *(He jumps out the window, disappearing.)*

LUCY. Help, help! Doctor Van Helsing!

> *(Music in.*)*

---

*A license to produce *DRACULA: A COMEDY OF TERRORS* does not include a performance license for any third-party or copyrighted recordings. Licensees should create their own.

Scene Seven

VAN HELSING. 22nd October, 1897. Mina Westfeldt is missing. And there is only one logical suspect: Renfield. Clearly his appetite for insects has grown to a thirst for human blood.

(Sound effects: Musical sting.)

(Westfeldt home, the drawing room – the following day.)

DR. WESTFELDT. Men! Our search for Renfield has thus far yielded nothing! We must redouble our efforts. There are horses, pitchforks and amphetamines outside. For the good of Whitby, for the good of England, let's kill that monster – and bring back my *second favorite daughter*!

(Sound effects: The men disperse.)

LUCY. We'll find them, father.

DR. WESTFELDT. I'm not so certain. The men have been searching for days.

VAN HELSING. Maybe you should've asked some women.

DR. WESTFELDT. I'm going back out to liaise with the other search parties. I need backup.

LUCY. Jonathan?

*(**HARKER** eats a mini egg salad sandwich.)*

HARKER. *(Mouth full.)* Huh?

LUCY. My father needs help.

HARKER. And I would be happy to, but you know I'm useless with a pitchfork. Wouldn't want to hurt anyone. Or myself. Splinters.

LUCY. *(Disappointed.)* Of course.

VAN HELSING. I'll back you up, Wallace.

DR. WESTFELDT. Very kind of you Jean, but –

VAN HELSING. I've had three children, buried two husbands, and I benchpress 127 Kilos. I think I can handle myself, thank you.

(She exits, followed by an impressed **DR. WESTFELDT**.*)*

DR. WESTFELDT. Very well, then.

HARKER. *(Sheepish, careful.)* Lucy, are you alright?

LUCY. Sure.

HARKER. Dr. Van Helsing had it well in hand. But next time –

LUCY. *(Quietly.)* Next time we need someone to step up, we'll be sure to look for Doctor Van Helsing.

HARKER. Lucy, that's not fair.

LUCY. I guess it's just not who you are.

HARKER. Not yet, but I'm working on it.

LUCY. Right.

HARKER. You know I love you, don't you?

LUCY. Yes.

HARKER. You're the most wonderful thing that's ever happened to me.

LUCY. I need to be alone for a while, if you don't mind.

HARKER. Do you want some company?

LUCY. Jonathan.

HARKER. *(Off* **LUCY**'s *look.)* Right.

(He leaves. As soon as he's off –)

(Sound effects: Woosh.)

(Out of thin air, **COUNT DRACULA** *appears.)*

DRACULA. Lucy.

LUCY. Count! You're alright! Thank heavens. I feared Renfield must have gotten to you too.

DRACULA. *(Quick thinking.)* He did. But I made a narrow escape.

LUCY. The men just left. Would you like a finger sandwich?

DRACULA. Thank you, but I had a bite in Saltwick Park on my way over.

LUCY. There are restaurants in Saltwick Park?

DRACULA. Lucy, I needed to see you again. To be near you. I have thought of nothing else since we last spoke.

(He leans in to kiss her. **LUCY** *tries to resist but is under his spell.)*

LUCY. I'm engaged to be married. This is inappropriate. Dangerous even.

DRACULA. And you are drawn to danger, are you not?

LUCY. Within reason.

DRACULA. Reason has nothing to do with it. We're the same, you and me. You're excited right now, aren't you?

LUCY. Count, please.

DRACULA. I have been waiting for you for centuries, and suddenly here you are, everything I dreamed. That's why I came to Whitby – for you. That's why I bought Withering Manor – for you. Why I turned my life upside down – not that it's an uncomfortable position for me – *for you!* I can't pretend we weren't meant for each other, and you know you can't either. Be my bride, Lucy. Stand next to me, preferably on my left because I've been told my right is more attractive.

LUCY. This is insane. I have to go –

DRACULA. Not yet.

>   *(He grabs her by the arm.)*

LUCY. Let go of me! Please!

>   *(He controls her arms, which move to his chest.)*

DRACULA. Why? Because it feels good? You said it yourself. Venture past your fears.

>   *(Her hands move to his butt.)*

LUCY. But... but...

DRACULA. Live in the present.

>   *(He kisses her. She lets him, for a beat more than she should. Then:)*

LUCY. Stop it! Stop it now! This is wrong. Jonathan –

DRACULA. Is a coward. You know what you want, what you need. Come with me. I can give you an extraordinary life.

>   *(**HARKER** approaches.)*

HARKER. Lucy, I'm so sorry to...interrupt. But your father is back with some news.

LUCY. Have they found Mina?

HARKER. I don't believe so, but he's asking for you.

LUCY. I'll go find him.

DRACULA. Will I...see you later?

LUCY. *(Conflicted.)* It's a small town.

>   *(She exits.)*

DRACULA. *(To **HARKER**.)* I should be going as well.

> (**DRACULA** *flourishes his cape, as if to magically disappear himself, then:)*

HARKER. Wait. Count Dracula, might I have a word?

DRACULA. Absolutely. Tomorrow.

> (**DRACULA** *tries again, then:)*

HARKER. *(In pain, in need of help.)* Please. Just a moment of your time.

DRACULA. Very well. What is it?

HARKER. Yes, I was wondering. How is it that you can be so... so brazen? So fearless in life?

DRACULA. You think I'm fearless?

HARKER. Of course. Look at you. What could you possibly be afraid of?

DRACULA. More than you know. But fear is temporary. Regret is forever.

HARKER. You'll think this is silly, but I have a... a sort of... voice in my head that tells me when I'm going to get hurt.

DRACULA. Ah, the voice of self-preservation. Fight or flight.

HARKER. Guess which one I choose?

DRACULA. *(Seductive.)* It can be tempting to run from an uncomfortable feeling, sure. But if you ignore it, you'll never know the sweet taste of what's on the other side.

HARKER. What's that?

DRACULA. Accomplishment, pride, satisfaction.

> (*They are close.)*

HARKER. You're really cool, you know that?

DRACULA. The question is, do you know how cool *you* are?

        (DRACULA leans in.)

HARKER. *(Pulling away.)* I'm not cool. I'm the opposite of cool.

DRACULA. Which makes you...hot? You're highly kissable.

HARKER. I...uh...hahaha. You're joking, right?

DRACULA. Not even a little. Are you not curious?

HARKER. Somewhat. But I could never see myself actually doing anything about it.

DRACULA. Imagine getting married without knowing yourself fully.

HARKER. Do I have a choice?

DRACULA. You always have a choice.

HARKER. But I could never really – never actually –

        (DRACULA kisses HARKER.)

Well that wasn't...terrible.

DRACULA. Aw, gee thanks. Jonathan you're capable of so much more than you know. You can be anyone you want. You can be *with* anyone you want. Doesn't have to be Lucy.

HARKER. But it will be Lucy! She's my "meant to be."

DRACULA. Maybe, maybe not... now if you'll excuse me, I gotta fly!

        (DRACULA swirls his cape but...)

        (Sound effects: Crunch!)

        (Nothing. He is still there.)

Sorry. Wardrobe malfunction. I'll just be going then, with my feet...

(He exits the long way, trying to maintain dignity.)

Bye, bye.

*(**DR. WESTFELDT** and **VAN HELSING** enter with urgency.)*

VAN HELSING. Jonathan!

HARKER. What's wrong?

DR. WESTFELDT. Where's Lucy?

(Calling to her.)

Lucy!

*(**LUCY** runs back in.)*

LUCY. What is it father?

DR. WESTFELDT. Thank God you're safe!

LUCY. What's happened?

DR. WESTFELDT. Apparently, there was another attack in town this evening.

(Music in.)*

It happened near Saltwick Park.

LUCY. Saltwick Park?

VAN HELSING. Just an hour ago. The girl had the same marks on her neck.

HARKER. How gruesome.

LUCY. Did you speak with her?

VAN HELSING. Unfortunately, the girl is dead.

---

* A license to produce *DRACULA: A COMEDY OF TERRORS* does not include a performance license for any third-party or copyrighted recordings. Licensees should create their own.

LUCY. So quickly?

VAN HELSING. She was hit by a horse and carriage as she ran from her attacker.

DR. WESTFELDT. Renfield.

HARKER. He's still in Whitby?

LUCY. Are we certain that Renfield is the killer?

DR. WESTFELDT. Who else could it be? This is a small village, and I like to jump to *conclusions.*

VAN HELSING. Unless...

DR. WESTFELDT. Yes?

VAN HELSING. It would have to be someone we've only ever seen at night.

LUCY. Yes! *And* someone who's allergic to garlic.

VAN HELSING. You're getting warmer.

LUCY. And that captain's log mentioned bite marks on the corpses of those sailors.

VAN HELSING. And there was only one survivor.

HARKER. And?

DR. WESTFELDT. Good heavens, enough with the chit chat! What are you saying?!

VAN HELSING & LUCY. *Count Dracula is the vampire!*

(*Sound effects: Wolf howl.*)

DR. WESTFELDT. I can't believe how long it took us to figure that out.

(*They discuss internally for a moment, then –*)

LUCY. We must find him and free Mina at once!

VAN HELSING. And then destroy him before he strikes again.

DR. WESTFELDT. Lucy, you are to stay home.

LUCY. I want to come, father.

DR. WESTFELDT. Please. I've already lost one daughter. I could not bear to lose you. Kitty will stand guard.

HARKER. *(Summoning his nerve.)* I'll join you!

LUCY. You will?

DR. WESTFELDT. You will?

VAN HELSING. You will?

LUCY. Jonathan, it's alright. You don't need to go. Really.

HARKER. In sickness and in health.

LUCY. Please be careful.

HARKER. That may be the one thing you don't have to worry about.

VAN HELSING. Jonathan, grab a torch! We're going vampire hunting.

> *(Music.*)*

> *(Sound effects: Dogs barking, night owls.)*

---

* A license to produce *DRACULA: A COMEDY OF TERRORS* does not include a performance license for any third-party or copyrighted recordings. Licensees should create their own.

Scene Eight

(Sound effects: Horses gallop.)

(DR. WESTFELDT, VAN HELSING *and* **HARKER** *appear center stage with cheap children's toy horse head broomsticks between their legs and lanterns aloft – galloping.)*

VAN HELSING. We've not a minute to waste.

DR. WESTFELDT. We must save Mina's soul!

VAN HELSING. Yes, but be warned. She will be prone to violent behavior.

HARKER. Violent?

VAN HELSING. And anyone she bites will be cursed for all eternity.

HARKER. Come to think of it, this isn't quite safe. And tonight *is* laundry night –

DR. WESTFELDT. Pull it together, man! We must rescue Mina and put an end to this nasty business!

VAN HELSING. We're approaching the moors! I can feel it in the air.

DR. WESTFELDT, VAN HELSING & HARKER. *(Slowing the horses.)* Whoa, whoa...

(They stomp and make horse sounds, as they "arrive at the gates of the cemetery.")

DR. WESTFELDT. Withering Manor is just on the other side of this cemetery.

(Cemetery music in.)*

---

* A license to produce *DRACULA: A COMEDY OF TERRORS* does not include a performance license for any third-party or copyrighted recordings. Licensees should create their own.

HARKER. *(Terrified.)* It's awfully dark. You know what? Why don't you go *through* the cemetery while I scout the well-lit perimeter?

(**HARKER** *dashes off.*)

VAN HELSING. *(Spotting something.)* Do you see what I see? Fresh footprints.

DR. WESTFELDT. And an old box of baking powder.

VAN HELSING. He's clearly been here very recently.

DR. WESTFELDT. I say, you're a good sight cleverer than any woma– *(He stops, corrects himself.)* Any *doctor* I've met before. I am sorry for misjudging you when you first arrived.

VAN HELSING. That's quite alright, Wallace. It takes a very big man to admit his mistakes.

(*Beat.*)

Unt I happen to be partial to a very big man.

DR. WESTFELDT. Ah, I see.

(*Romantic music.**)

(**DR. WESTFELDT** *"clops" his horse closer to* **VAN HELSING**.)

Doctor Van Helsing. Perhaps when all this is over, we could see each other in a less...macabre context.

VAN HELSING. Ja. I vould like that.

(**VAN HELSING** *"clops" her horse closer to* **DR. WESTFELDT**.)

Und please, call me Jean.

---

* A license to produce *DRACULA: A COMEDY OF TERRORS* does not include a performance license for any third-party or copyrighted recordings. Licensees should create their own.

(*An elderly* **GRAVEDIGGER** *pops up with a shovel, spookily…*)

GRAVEDIGGER. (*Cockney.*) Careful, misses. Strange goings on in here tonight.

VAN HELSING. What do you mean?

DR. WESTFELDT. Grave robbers? Hooligans?

GRAVEDIGGER. No, sir. But most peculiar fing. I just started me night shift when I noticed what looked like a cape fluttering in the wind. I ran outside to see what it was, and I could have swore it were the grim reaper himself. All in black. And then suddenly, 'e just lifted off the ground and flew into the sky, like 'e was a bird or, or…a *bat* or somefink…

VAN HELSING. A bat? Are you sure?

GRAVEDIGGER. Troof be told, I am very drunk.

VAN HELSING. Still. Which way did he fly?

(**GRAVEDIGGER** *points.*)

GRAVEDIGGER. Towards Withering Manor.

VAN HELSING. Of course! Dracula!

DR. WESTFELDT. Thank you for your help, old man.

GRAVEDIGGER. I'm twenty-six.

(*Suspense music.**)

---

*A license to produce *DRACULA: A COMEDY OF TERRORS* does not include a performance license for any third-party or copyrighted recordings. Licensees should create their own.

Scene Nine

(Lucy's bedroom, immediately following. **LUCY** *is in her bed, asleep. It is the same bed as Mina's, but facing downstage.* **DRACULA** *appears upstage of the headboard, looking down at* **LUCY**.*)*

(Sound effects: Woosh.)

DRACULA. My queen, I have returned for you.

*(***LUCY*** stirs.)*

LUCY. *(Breathily.)* Jonathan –

DRACULA. It's not Jonathan.

(Seductive music.)*

*(***LUCY*** jumps out of bed.)*

LUCY. Count! Don't come any closer! I know all about you now.

DRACULA. Allow me to explain.

LUCY. Explain what you did to my sister? To that poor girl in Saltwick Park?

DRACULA. They meant nothing to me.

LUCY. That's even worse! And what about Kitty?

DRACULA. She's in a better place now.

LUCY. You killed her?!

DRACULA. What? No! I *hired* her. I give her benefits and weekends off!

(Sound effects: Thunder.)

---

* A license to produce *DRACULA: A COMEDY OF TERRORS* does not include a performance license for any third-party or copyrighted recordings. Licensees should create their own.

LUCY. Please leave at once!

DRACULA. I am the only one who truly loves you without reservation.

LUCY. You do not know the meaning of the word.

DRACULA. Reservation?

LUCY. No, love!!

DRACULA. What are you talking about? I have loved you since I first laid eyes on you.

(He moves toward **LUCY***, they tussle.)*

LUCY. Count, stop.

DRACULA. I cannot wait any longer. We will marry tonight!

LUCY. Tonight?!

(He lifts her.)

DRACULA. I have a ship waiting in port. And the wind is picking up.

LUCY. Let go of me! You're a monster! A vile beast!

(She frees herself.)

DRACULA. Do you not find me desirable? Because that would make me very unhappy. And when I am unhappy, I drink more than I should.

(Sound effects: Crunch.)

(He rips a piece of the bed off, unconscious of his own strength.)

You know I have a problem with impulse control. It would be a shame if something were to happen to your father.

LUCY. *(Calming him.)* No! Count, of course I desire you.

DRACULA. Let's be honest, it would be weird if you didn't, right? So you'll marry me?

LUCY. *(Staving him off.)* Yes. Uh huh.

>*(Beat.)*

But I need another day to get my affairs in order. I'll have to figure out how to tell Jonathan. This is going to break his heart.

DRACULA. Jonathan. Yes. He will be hurt, but he will be stronger for it.

>*(He goes in to kiss her, but then:)*

>*(Sound effects: Rooster.)*

>*(He pulls away dramatically.)*

It's almost dawn. I must away. Until sunset, my sweet.

>*(He disappears in a whirl.)*

>*(Sound effects: Thunder, music.*)*

---

* A license to produce *DRACULA: A COMEDY OF TERRORS* does not include a performance license for any third-party or copyrighted recordings. Licensees should create their own.

Scene Ten

(Withering Manor front door, foyer.)

(The front door slowly opens with a loud, long squeak. **VAN HELSING, HARKER, DR. WESTFELDT** *all stick their heads in cautiously.)*

VAN HELSING. Count Dracula!

DR. WESTFELDT. We demand to see you!

HARKER. So we can kill you!

VAN HELSING. *(Under her breath.)* Let's not lead with that.

> *(***KITTY** *approaches, holding a bird cage and feather duster.)*

KITTY. Blimey! You can't just go walking into people's – Oh, Mister Doctor Westfeldt.

DR. WESTFELDT. Kitty? What are you doing here? What has he done to you?

KITTY. Paid me a living wage is what he done. I no longer have to steal things!

DR. WESTFELDT. Is that our bird cage?

KITTY. *(Lying.)* No.

> *(She throws it offstage.)*

> *(Sound effects: Squawk, feathers fly.)*

VAN HELSING. Where is the Count?

DR. WESTFELDT. We demand to see him now!

> *(She continues to dust, avoiding them.)*

KITTY. I fink 'e said somefin' about sleeping in London today.

VAN HELSING. London! What has he done with Mina?

DR. WESTFELDT. We demand to see her too!

KITTY. Oh that mess? She's floating around here somewhere.

(She exits.)

DR. WESTFELDT. Wait! Kitty!

HARKER. That was rude.

VAN HELSING. We should split up into groups.

HARKER. Groups? There are only three of us.

VAN HELSING. Right. I'll go with Wallace.

DR. WESTFELDT. See you soon, Jonathan. Godspeed!

*(**DR. WESTFELDT** and **VAN HELSING** run off.)*

HARKER. But... but I thought –

(Sound effects: A bat swoops over his head. And another. Wind whips up, ghoulish sound of a woman giggling.)

Hello? Hello? Is someone there?

*(Sound effects: Fugue of **MINA** intoning "Jonathan.")*

*(Ghostly **MINA** crosses upstage of **HARKER** on a Razor scooter.*)*

Yes. That's me.

*(Sound effects: "Jonathan" fugue grows as **MINA** crosses again.)*

Is that you, Mina?

---

* A license to produce *DRACULA: A COMEDY OF TERRORS* does not include a license to publicly display any branded logos or trademarked images. Licensees must acquire rights for any logos and/or images or create their own.

(A bright light builds blinding **HARKER.***)*

HARKER. *(Screaming.)* MINAAAAA!

> *(Sound effects: Bat sounds, as from Dracula earlier.)*

> *(Blackout.)*

> *(Sound effects: Thunder, lightning. Howl in the distance.)*

> *(Back at the front door, a breathless* **LUCY** *runs in just as* **DR. WESTFELDT** *and* **VAN HELSING** *emerge, their clothing rumpled.)*

DR. WESTFELDT. Who screamed?! What's happening?!

LUCY. Father!

DR. WESTFELDT. Lucy?!

LUCY. Your necktie! It's all rumpled. Did someone try to bite you?

VAN HELSING. *(Flirtatious.)* It was more like a nibble.

LUCY. Oh...

DR. WESTFELDT. What are you doing here? I told you I didn't want you involved.

LUCY. Please father, I am the best hope we have for saving Mina and vanquishing the Count.

VAN HELSING. She's right, Wallace. He seems to have a thing for her.

LUCY. He wants to marry me. I agreed, but only to buy us a few more hours. Of course I would never marry that monster. If we don't do something, Mina will be lost forever and who knows what will become of Whitby.

DR. WESTFELDT. I don't understand you, child. Always running toward danger!

(She stands up to her father, her sense of duty is paramount.)

LUCY. I'm a Westfeldt, damnit! Helping people is in our blood. No matter the consequence.

DR. WESTFELDT. You're just as stubborn as your mother was.

LUCY. Please. Let me fight for my sister.

(He takes a breath.)

DR. WESTFELDT. You care so deeply.

(Beat.)

And you're right. We can't do this without you.

LUCY. Thank you.

(She hugs him, they are both moved.)

DR. WESTFELDT. My darling, you've no idea how very proud I am of the woman you have become. Your mother would be as well.

LUCY. Oh, father.

(Suddenly realizing –)

Where's Jonathan?

*(Sound effects: Electric guitar shred… **HARKER** arrives, now in leather pants and unbuttoned shirt, a la Dracula's look.)*

HARKER. *(Austin Powers.)* Right here, baby.

LUCY. Are those…leather trousers?

HARKER. You like the lace-up crotch?

LUCY. Wow. I don't hate it.

VAN HELSING. Look! Bite marks on his neck!

HARKER. Nice right? Mina says hi, by the way.

LUCY. Jonathan, did you and Mina –?

HARKER. Don't worry babe, it was just an innocent bite, followed by an innocent suck.

LUCY. I beg your pardon!

HARKER. On the neck! You should be proud. I ventured past my fears. Wayyy past.

> (**HARKER** *opens his mouth wide toward them, exposing fangs.*)
>
> (*Sound effects: Bat screech.*)
>
> (**LUCY, VAN HELSING** *and* **DR. WESTFELDT** *sidebar.*)

LUCY. What do we do, Doctor?

VAN HELSING. The only way to save Jonathan is to kill the vampire that infected him.

LUCY. Mina?!

VAN HELSING. Indeed. Unless...

LUCY. Unless?

VAN HELSING. Unless we kill the vampire that infected Mina. Then Jonathan will be free as well.

DR. WESTFELDT. It's like a pyramid scheme.

VAN HELSING. Correct. We must go to London and find Dracula now.

DR. WESTFELDT. London is a big city.

LUCY. Jonathan sold him five properties there. He must be in one of them.

VAN HELSING. Excellent. If we manage to locate Dracula before he wakes at sunset, we can open his coffin, drive a stake through his heart and end this scourge once and for all.

LUCY. To London!

ALL. To London!

> *(Sound effects: Suspense music,* horses gallop at a pace, the rickety sound of a carriage.)*

---

* A license to produce *DRACULA: A COMEDY OF TERRORS* does not include a performance license for any third-party or copyrighted recordings. Licensees should create their own.

Scene Eleven

(Two benches become a carriage, the higher one in back becoming the rumble seat for **LUCY** *and* **HARKER**, *who sit with a blanket covering their laps. In front,* **DR. WESTFELDT** *and* **VAN HELSING** *consult a map of London.)*

HARKER. I say! It's awfully bumpy, isn't it?

LUCY. Shall I ask them to slow the horses?

HARKER. Hell, no! It's bloody good fun! Let's live on the edge.

LUCY. If you say so.

(He leans in and kisses her like in a movie. She pulls away, excited by his newfound confidence.)

Jonathan! What has gotten into you?

HARKER. Vampire blood, I assume.

LUCY. You're terrible. Let's do it again.

(She goes in for more. They make out passionately.)

DR. WESTFELDT. We want to get to him before he rises at dusk.

VAN HELSING. We should travel from east to west to beat the sunset.

DR. WESTFELDT. We'll start in Greenwich, then on to Westminster and so on.

*(***LUCY*** looks forward, wipes her mouth.)*

LUCY. Doctor? Is there any way we might keep him like this, just a little?

VAN HELSING. I'm afraid not, Lucy.

LUCY. Then I'd better get my kicks in now.

> (*She and* **HARKER** *pull the blanket up over them, as they lower behind the front "seat." We hear them going at it.*)

DR. WESTFELDT. I'd rather not be hearing this.

VAN HELSING. Just sing with me, Wallace.

DR. WESTFELDT & VAN HELSING.
GOD SAVE OUR GRACIOUS QUEEN,
LONG LIVE OUR NOBLE QUEEN,
GOD SAVE THE QUEEN!

> (*As they sing, we see a pair of puppet "Lucy legs" complete with boots and lacy stockings, pop up from behind the blanket as if she is upside down – opening and closing and contorting into impossible angles.*)

> (*From under the blanket, we hear climax sounds into:*)

> (*Sound effects: Church bells.*)

Scene Twelve

(Greenwich row house, front door.)

VAN HELSING. This must be it. The map shows the Cutty Sark just across the street.

DR. WESTFELDT. That gargoyle looks ominous.

VAN HELSING. The mark of the vampire. He is surely inside.

DR. WESTFELDT. Look at that sign.

LUCY. *(Reading.)* Deliveries in the rear – only accepted after sunset.

HARKER. Kinky.

DR. WESTFELDT. Let me at that miscreant now.

VAN HELSING. Tread carefully, Wallace.

(Sound effects: Door open.)

Empty!

LUCY. I can smell his cologne. He must be here.

VAN HELSING. Search the bedrooms!

HARKER. The Count was more interested in the basement. Right this way. It's a few flights down.

> *(Music in as they pretend to walk down an invisible flight of stairs.* They arrive at a landing. Music out.)*

Down we go!

VAN HELSING. Of course. He wants to be as far from the sun's rays as possible.

(Music in as they pretend to walk down another invisible flight of stairs. They arrive at the next landing. Music out.)*

HARKER. Just a few more!

DR. WESTFELDT. How many? We must be under the Thames by now.

(Music in as they pretend to walk down another invisible flight of stairs. They arrive at the next landing. Music out.)*

HARKER. Last one!

(Music in, they all grumble as they pretend to walk down another invisible flight of stairs, as the lights go completely out. Music out.)*

(Sound effects: Water drips, rats, basement sounds.)

Here we are.

DR. WESTFELDT. Does someone have a match? I can hardly see a thing.

LUCY. I think I feel a candle.

HARKER. That's not a candle.

LUCY. Jonathan!

VAN HELSING. But *this* is.

(She lights a candle, revealing a coffin.)

(They all gasp.)

Jonathan, quickly! The stake!

(**HARKER** *pulls out a stake.*)

HARKER. Ready!

VAN HELSING. Alright, Wallace. I want you to open slowly the coffin.

DR. WESTFELDT. Ready.

VAN HELSING. On the count of three.

LUCY. Heaven help us.

HARKER. With this blow, I extinguish the dark flames of evil that have burned for centuries.

VAN HELSING. Okay.

ALL. One!

(*Beat.*)

Two!

(*Painful beat.*)

Two and a half –

(*Finally.*)

Three!

(**DR. WESTFELDT** *throws open the coffin lid, which opens downstage toward the audience, so we cannot see inside.* **HARKER** *repeatedly and violently stabs his stake into the coffin –*)

HARKER. (*Vengeful passion.*) Ahhhh! Die, you blood sucking bane of the planet! Die! Die! Die! Die! Die!

(*Beat.*)

He's not in there.

VAN HELSING. He must be at one of the other properties.

DR. WESTFELDT. To Westminster!

ALL. Montage!

> *(Sound effects: Wind shear.)*

> *(As they all run downstage and jump, landing in:)*

> *(Westminster apartment.)*

HARKER. He said he wanted a view of Big Ben.

DR. WESTFELDT. Can't get much closer than this.

LUCY. There's the coffin!

VAN HELSING. You know the drill.

ALL. One! Two! Two and a Half! Three!

> (**LUCY** *throws open a coffin lid on the other side of the stage.*)

HARKER. Empty again!

DR. WESTFELDT. To Piccadilly Circus!

> *(Sound effects: Wind shear.)*

> *(As they all run downstage and jump, landing in:)*

> *(Piccadilly Circus apartment.)*

HARKER. The flat is just above the old Shaftesbury Theatre.

VAN HELSING. What's playing?

HARKER. *Mamma Mia.*

VAN HELSING. Here we go again!

ALL. Onetwothree!

HARKER. Nothing!

DR. WESTFELDT. To Knightsbridge!

> *(Sound effects: Wind shear.)*
>
> *(As they all run downstage and jump, landing in:)*
>
> *(Knightsbridge.)*

He wasn't there, but we did buy some beautiful clothing at Harrods!

VAN HELSING. We've been through all the properties. Only one remains.

DR. WESTFELDT. To Abbey Road!

> *(Sound effects: Wind shear.)*
>
> *(Abbey Road.)*
>
> *(They jump up, landing in position, approximating the Beatles' album cover photo.)*

LUCY. Abbey Road.

HARKER. It certainly is long and winding.

DR. WESTFELDT. With a spiffy view of the Octopus' Garden in the shade.

VAN HELSING. We get it. The Beatles. Let it be!

> **(DR. WESTFELDT** *spins around, adds wig and lowers pipe to become* **RENFIELD.**)

RENFIELD. Did someone say beetles?

ALL. Renfield!

HARKER. Stay away from her! I command you.

VAN HELSING. What have you done with Wallace?

RENFIELD. I don't know what you're talking about.

(He spins around, removes wig, raises pipe to become **DR. WESTFELDT**.*)*

DR. WESTFELDT. Just gone to the loo. Popping out for a smoke now. Won't be a moment.

(He spins around, adds wig to become **RENFIELD**.*)*

LUCY. Renfield, where have you been?

RENFIELD. At the mercy of the Count.

VAN HELSING. Well it ends now.

(He spins around, removes wig, raises pipe to become **DR. WESTFELDT**.*)*

DR. WESTFELDT. And my dear Mina can return to us.

(He spins around, adds wig and lowers pipe to become **RENFIELD**.*)*

RENFIELD. Will you take me back, Doctor? Can you ever forgive my trespasses?

(He spins around, removes wig, raises pipe to become **DR. WESTFELDT**.*)*

DR. WESTFELDT. Of course, James, of course.

(He spins around, adds wig and lowers pipe to become **RENFIELD**.*)*

RENFIELD. Bless you, doctor!

(He spins around, removes wig, raises pipe to become **DR. WESTFELDT**.*)*

DR. WESTFELDT. *(Out of breath, unsteady.)* My pleasure. Anyone else dizzy?

*(***HARKER*** *opens and slams a coffin door.)*

HARKER. Bollocks, nothing again!

DR. WESTFELDT. Where can he be?

VAN HELSING. You sold him five properties in London, correct?

HARKER. Correct! We've seen them all.

LUCY. *(A light bulb.)* All the *properties*, perhaps, but not all the *coffins*.

VAN HELSING. What do you mean?

LUCY. The ship's manifest! It listed *six* coffins.

HARKER. Six? But that means the last coffin –

LUCY. Is back at Withering Manor. He must have been sleeping there all along.

HARKER. I don't understand. Kitty said –

DR. WESTFELDT. Kitty is a compulsive liar.

VAN HELSING. I thought she was a kleptomaniac.

DR. WESTFELDT. Mental health is an inexact science.

LUCY. We've got to get there before sunset!

ALL. To Withering Manor!

(Sound effects: Very short woosh.)

(They take a small step forward.)

DR. WESTFELDT. We made excellent time.

(Withering Manor.)

LUCY. This way! Toward the crypt!

(Music.)*

---

*A license to produce *DRACULA: A COMEDY OF TERRORS* does not include a performance license for any third-party or copyrighted recordings. Licensees should create their own.

(They turn on themselves, marching down invisible stairs. As they progress, it becomes hazier and more mysterious.)

DR. WESTFELDT. The sun is almost down.

VAN HELSING. He will soon wake from his slumber.

HARKER. We must screw our courage to the sticking place, all of us!

(As they reach the crypt, it is filled with low-lying fog. Dracula's large and ornate coffin is dramatically revealed.)

(Big music.)*

(Intense whisper.) Based on that music, this has to be it!

ALL. *(Terrified.)* One! Two... Two and a half –

*(The coffin lid opens, revealing **DRACULA** waking up, perhaps in a sleep mask.)*

DRACULA. *(Loud yawn.)* Aaaeeaw!

DR. WESTFELDT. Count Dracula!

HARKER. Prepare to meet your doom!

*(Woosh! **DRACULA** magically pulls the stake from **HARKER**.)*

DRACULA. Not today, I'm getting married.

*(He sees **LUCY**.)*

Lucy!

VAN HELSING. You wretched creature! You're not going anywhere near Lucy. Or Jonathan!

DR. WESTFELDT. Or my patient, Renfield.

*(He spins around, adds wig, lowers pipe to become **RENFIELD**.)*

RENFIELD. Or my doctor.

(He spins around, removes wig, raises pipe to become **DR. WESTFELDT**.*)*

DR. WESTFELDT. Or Jean Van Helsing.

VAN HELSING. Or Renfield.

DR. WESTFELDT. We covered him already.

VAN HELSING. Right.

DR. WESTFELDT. Or Mina!

*(***VAN HELSING*** *spins around and holds* **MINA** *wig on head.)*

MINA. You remembered!

(She spins back around, removes wig to become **VAN HELSING**.*)*

DR. WESTFELDT. Or Kitty!

*(***LUCY*** *spins around, holds* **KITTY**'s *maid's hat on head.)*

KITTY. So sweet of you to think of me. I'm just a peripheral character.

(She spins back around, removes maid's hat to become **LUCY**.*)*

DRACULA. Enough!

(Crossing to her.) Lucy, let's go. I want the world to know how much I care about you. That's right!

(Jumps up on a bench.)

I love Lucy!

LUCY. But I don't love you!

DRACULA. What?

LUCY. I'm sorry I lied but you threatened my family, I had no choice. I'm not going anywhere with you.

DRACULA. I love when we fight, it's like we're already married!

LUCY. Are you not listening? We are never ever going to be together.

DRACULA. Alright, fine. I'm flexible.

(Then.)

Jonathan? Can I interest you in eternal life?

HARKER. I've already found the one for me. She's everything I need. The love of my life.

DRACULA. I see.

(Beat, grasping.)

How about the three of us? Maybe we explore a new kind of –

HARKER. Count, stop performing! The only person you actually love is the one in the mirror.

DRACULA. Doesn't really apply, but I get what you're going for.

LUCY. Love is selfless. Have you managed even one selfless act in your entire life? That's the difference between you and Jonathan.

DRACULA. *That's* the difference?!

LUCY. It wasn't easy for him, but he worked past his fears. And he did it for me. You've had so many lifetimes, and still you're not happy.

(He is silent.)

It makes me wonder if too much time is just as bad as not enough. I mean, is there anything left that you want?

DRACULA. Yes. I want... I want...what you and Jonathan have.

LUCY. *(Truly surprised.)* You do?

DRACULA. Yes. Look at you two; living proof that real love doesn't have to be sexy.

> (**LUCY** *and* **HARKER** *take in the backhanded compliment.)*

So if that means going so far as to put someone else's needs before my own, I'm ready.

LUCY. Then here's your chance! Mina and Jonathan are innocent. Let them go, I beg of you. Make our family whole again.

DRACULA. I wish I could, Lucy. But once bitten, they are cursed forever, unless...

LUCY. Unless?

DRACULA. The only way I could release them from the curse would be to... to...

VAN HELSING. To die.

> (**DRACULA** *looks at* **VAN HELSING**. *He gets it.)*

DRACULA. Yes.

> *(Swallows.)*

> *(Dramatic music.*)*

Jonathan, you said you wanted to be brazen. To be fearless.

HARKER. I don't understand.

DRACULA. I need you to help me commit the first selfless act of my endless life.

---

*A license to produce *DRACULA: A COMEDY OF TERRORS* does not include a performance license for any third-party or copyrighted recordings. Licensees should create their own.

HARKER. How?

DRACULA. By ending it.

> (**DRACULA** *kisses his forehead lovingly, then crosses up to his coffin.*)

HARKER. Wait, you *want* me to... to...?

DRACULA. Kill me.

> (**DRACULA** *gasps and bares his chest, a target for* **HARKER***'s stake.*)

You'll have given me the best gift imaginable: Purpose. What do you say? Let's do this for each other.

HARKER. Very well, then.

> (**HARKER** *extends his arm up with the stake, looks at* **DRACULA***, then deflates.*)

I can't do it! I'm not like you. I cannot bear to take another life, no matter how monstrous.

DRACULA. Technically, I'm already dead.

HARKER. Still –

DRACULA. Did I mention I'm bankrupt? All those cheques are gonna bounce.

> (*Sound effects: Acid guitar sounds, bat cries.*)

> (*In slow motion, strobes and smoke,* **HARKER** *pushes* **DRACULA** *back into the coffin.*)

HARKER. DIE, YOU SON OF A –!

> (**HARKER** *stabs* **DRACULA** *in the heart, the stomach and then invites* **LUCY** *to join him for the final stab in* **DRACULA***'s crotch as confetti flies out.*)

> (*Sound effects: Thunder.*)

DRACULA. *(Weakly.)* It is done. And so am I.

> (**DRACULA** *disappears into the coffin, which emits smoke and sparks,* **HARKER** *closes the coffin door,* **LUCY** *meets him in front of coffin and they strike a triumphant tableau. They kiss.)*
>
> *(Sound effects: Church bells.)*

Epilogue

VAN HELSING. 7th July, 1898. Almost nine months have passed and things have finally returned to normal at the Westfeldt home. Mina spent several months convalescing in the hospital, where she met and fell in love with her physician, a Dr. Jekyll.

*(**DR. WESTFELDT** joins **VAN HELSING**.)*

Dr. Westfeldt has given up his practice to join me in the pursuit of the supernatural and a cozy domestic partnership.

(They rub noses adorably.)

Renfield is still a masochist, and Kitty is still a pathological liar. They now have successful careers in politics. Lucy became a guest lecturer at the Royal Geological Society and soon discovered that her bumpy carriage ride with Jonathan yielded an unexpected bump of its own, which she showed with pride on their wedding day.

*(**DR. WESTFELDT** and **VAN HELSING** throw white flower petals which float to the stage and become an aisle for the wedding procession.)*

*(A very pregnant **LUCY** appears in a wedding dress. **HARKER** is returned to his former self; glasses, bad hair, careful disposition.)*

*(Music: Vivaldi's "Four Seasons (Spring)." *)*

HARKER. Watch it darling, don't want to step on your train!

LUCY. Jonathan, I'm fine.

HARKER. But the floor is slick.

---

* A license to produce *DRACULA: A COMEDY OF TERRORS* does not include a performance license for any third-party or copyrighted recordings. Licensees should create their own.

LUCY. I must confess, although there is no one I would rather spend the rest of my days with, I sometimes... miss the old you. The *new* old you. The you before you went back to being –

HARKER. I thought you might say that. Which is why I brought a cape for later.

LUCY. *(Titillated.)* Oh, Jonathan.

>　　*(Music: Wedding march.)*

>　　*(A* **MINISTER** *appears upstage, face hidden under a large monk's hood, looking down into a bible.)*

It's funny, it seems that in order to truly learn how to live, we had to almost die.

HARKER. Lucy Westfeldt, I'd rather share one lifetime with you than eternity with everyone else.

LUCY. *(Holding stomach.)* Oof! Darling, the baby, the baby!

HARKER. What is it?

LUCY. I just felt a kick!

HARKER. How wonderful!

LUCY. Or was it...a *bite*?

>　　*(Music in: Bach's "Toccata and Fugue in D minor," organ.*)*

>　　*(The* **MINISTER** *pulls back the hood. It's* **DRACULA,** *laughing wildly.* **LUCY, HARKER, DR. WESTFELDT** *and* **VAN HELSING** *reveal they all have vampire teeth as the music crests. Blackout.)*

Fin

---

* A license to produce *DRACULA: A COMEDY OF TERRORS* does not include a performance license for any third-party or copyrighted recordings. Licensees should create their own.

www.ingramcontent.com/pod-product-compliance
Lightning Source LLC
Chambersburg PA
CBHW070341120726
47909CB00008B/2712